3X KRAZY 2

De'Kari

Lock Down Publications & Ca$h Presents

3X KRAZY 2
A Novel by *De'Kari*

De'Kari

Lock Down Publications

P.O. Box 944
Stockbridge, Ga 30281

Visit our website at www.lockdownpublications.com

Cover design and layout by: **Dynasty's Cover Me**
Book interior design by: **Shawn Walker**
Edited by: **Kiera Northington**

Stay Connected with Us!

Text **LOCKDOWN** to 22828 to stay up-to-date with new releases, sneak peaks, contests and more…

Thanks

Submission Guideline

Submit the first three chapters of your completed manuscript to ldpsubmissions@gmail.com, subject line: Your book's title. The manuscript must be in a .doc file and sent as an attachment. Document should be in Times New Roman, double spaced and in size 12 font. Also, provide your synopsis and full contact information. If sending multiple submissions, they must each be in a separate email.

Have a story but no way to send it electronically? You can still submit to LDP/Ca$h Presents. Send in the first three chapters, written or typed, of your completed manuscript to:

LDP: Submissions Dept
P.O. Box 944
Stockbridge, Ga 30281

*DO NOT send original manuscript. Must be a duplicate. *

Provide your synopsis and a cover letter containing your full contact information.

Thanks for considering LDP and Ca$h Presents.

THANKS

Thanks to all my supporters, readers, fans, critics, and everybody in between. If it wasn't for you, none of this would be possible and I would just be another convict with a story to tell. Instead, thanks to all of you, they now call me King of Cali. I don't know if I've earned that title, but it sure sounds great.

A special thank you goes out to all the book clubs, the many that have done author spotlights on me. All the Die Hard's, y'all keep doing YOU, while we do US, cause this is Team De'Kari all the way!

To Ca$h and the Lockdown Family, "Damn it feels good to be the best!" Let's keep this shit moving and keep giving the readers something to love.

Butterfly, I see you Lil Mama. "We all we got!"

King De'Kari

De'Kari

PROLOGUE

TASHA

I exited my Lexus truck on the dark, stormy night with my mind made up. My intentions weren't necessarily clear, but my actions were. I'd been seated in my truck, parked outside the church for over twenty minutes, preparing myself mentally to face the truth.

I was wearing a nice pair of six-inch Jimmy Choo's and a black Fendi leather trench coat. Underneath the coat, I was as naked as the day I was born. Naked as a jay bird!

Now was the time. I entered the church through the back, side door. It was a door I'd used plenty of times before. The door led directly into the corridor into the reverend's private chambers.

When I got to his office, he was seated at his desk awaiting my arrival, like I'd known he would be. When Rev. Jacobs saw me, a spark ignited in his eyes. My guess, the spark was from the anticipation of what we were about to do. What we've been doing since I was nine years old.

"Ah! Yes, my lovely, lovely angel, Tasha. How are you doing this beautiful evening, the Lord our God has blessed us with?" he asked me in his most sweet and sincere voice. The sick fuck had the nerves to use the Lord's name with evil intentions.

"I'm fine, Daddy, now that I am here with you." He's been having me call him Daddy for years now, whenever we are alone. Ever since he stole my innocence. However, calling him that now, at this moment, felt quite weird. Especially after finding out the reverend is my biological father.

As I walked over to him, he scooted his chair back some, making room for me on his lap. This was our normal routine.

Every time I came to his chambers, we would begin like this. I couldn't believe this was my father. This was the man who was supposed to love and protect me from the many evils of the world. Instead he was one of the world's most hideous demons preying up on my purity. Draining me, of my essence. He belonged on the front of the *Megan's Law* website.

"Daddy, I have something I need to tell you," I whispered in his ear as my tongue slid across his lobe.

His rough, strong hands were already hungrily roaming freely underneath my coat, rubbing across my body.

"What is it, Angel?" He asked me.

"I'm pregnant." I felt his body tense up underneath me.

"Isn't this wonderful news? Now we'll have proof of our love." I caught him completely off guard. I was no fool, there was no love between a rapist and his victim. Only a grave injustice.

Not anymore!

I kissed my way down to his neck. Then I made my way over to his other ear. His dry hand cupped and squeezed my ass, while the other fondled my breast.

I couldn't take it any longer!

His touch made my skin crawl as if a thousand centipedes were under its surface.

It was now or never! I slid the razor blade from beneath my tongue, the cold steel matching the ice in my veins.

"Revenge Is Promised, Daddy!" I whispered into his ear.

In one swift motion, I clenched the razor blade in my teeth and slid it across his monstrous throat. The blood burst from his carotid artery, spraying across my naked flesh. It was hot and thick, reminding me of the times he sprayed his semen across my chest.

His eyes got as big as silver dollars. His grip on my ass was like a vice until the life oozed out of his body, along with his blood.

"Bye, Daddy. We all know the truth now," I told him before making my way back out of the church the same way I entered.

Once I was back out in the night chill, the rain was coming down in a torrent. I took my coat off and stood there in the nude with my head tilted back. The rain washed away all traces of blood on my impregnated body, but not off of my soul.

"Keep it on the real, high siders / If you're real wit me, I'll be real wit you, yeah / 3X's Krazy / got your mind blown too /"

Minutes later, I was inside my truck driving along, wondering how I was going to tell Jeffrey, my fiancé and brother, that I was pregnant by our father.

*** 3X ***

De'Kari

CHAPTER 1

TASHA

For the life of me, I don't remember how I made it back home. The entire ride, I was tear-stained, and grief stricken. I felt stiff and sore all over, like I was laid out in the street just awakening from getting hit by a Mack truck, instead of waking up in my bed at home.

"Aarrgh!" What the fuck was that? An unbearable pain just shot down my side. It was so strong, if it happened again, I was likely to pass right out.

Beep! Beep! Beep! Beep!

"You think she's woke? Get help! Babe, are you okay? Tasha can you hear me?"

Why the fuck was Jeff in my room yelling in my ear? And what was that God-awful beeping sound?

"Tasha! Baby, it's okay. You're going to be okay." It was Jeffrey again. But why was he saying that to me?

"Jeff, babe, I'm o-okay. W-why are you yelling though?" My voice sounded like something out of a scary movie.

"Hold on, baby. The doctor should be here any minute."

"Did he just say doctor?"

That was how I woke up out of my coma two weeks ago and I still couldn't believe everything I was told. Apparently, I was so irate, I'd lost control of my Lexus and ran a red light. I was blindsided by a Yukon and ended up wrapped around a telephone pole.

But wait a minute now, I need to back up a little bit. For the last couple of weeks, I'd been feeling nauseated, but only during the early parts of the day. Fearing the worst, I took a home pregnancy test which confirmed my fears, I was pregnant. I couldn't feel joy about the baby because the baby was not my fiancé's, it was my father's. The father that had been molesting and raping me at church for the past eleven years.

The day I found out I was pregnant was the same day Jeffrey found out the truth about Jay. Wow! That was some more crazy shit! Finding out Mama J. had her own son killed at the hands of Uncle Bernard. Even still, the hardest pill to swallow per se was the fact that Rev. Jacobs had been molesting and raping girls for a long time, him and Uncle Bernard.

I heard one of the deacons found the reverend's body the following morning and of course, the church was making a big deal of it. That was expected. Along with the fact that they covered up him being found in his boxer shorts with his dick out.

Now, getting back to present time. I asked my doctor if I could speak to him in private. I wasn't trying to be rude, I just had something I wanted to discuss with him privately. It turns out there was no longer a need for privacy, the doctor had already informed Jeffrey that I was pregnant.

It turns out, the severe cramps I was feeling was my body trying to abort the baby. The doctor and his team were doing everything they could to prevent that.

Jeffrey shared with me that he had confronted my mother about all the lies, just as he had Mama J. From what he said, it was very intense. I knew I couldn't live under my mother's roof any longer. Not with me finding out everything she told me was a lie. From whom my father was, to the truth about God and His house. Yeah, fucking right!

Jeffrey ended up getting us a place to live off 16th and Chestnut Street. Not too far from Marston Campbell Park in Oakland. A nice two-bedroom, one and a half bath apartment. Jeffrey told me to spare no expense when it came to furniture and decorations, and I didn't.

I was admiring my beautiful handiwork after decorating the apartment when Jeffrey called to tell me he was outside.

*** **3X** ***

TO DA LEFT

I'd just gotten off the phone with Tasha as I pulled up to our new apartment. My cell phone began ringing the moment I put my Infiniti M45 in park.

"Dollar-Sign, what's good?" I called out to my best friend and brother after answering the phone.

"I'm the bearer of bad news, dog. Mothafuckas just tried to kill Abel. Shot 'em all the fuck up over at one of his bitch's houses," Dollar-Sign responded into the phone.

"What! Was it a set-up?"

"All I know is they killed the little bitch he was with. She caught like four slugs in the shootout."

"So, nigga, why you all calm and shit?" Ever since we killed Uncle Bernard, Dollar-Sign had been acting weird. He would be mumbling to himself or sometimes, he'd just start laughing for no reason.

"Aaa-ha-ha! You already know To Da Left, how I do when it's time. I'mma show up and show the fuck out. But until then, we must remain focused." As he was speaking, Tasha came walking outside.

I immediately got out of the car, standing on point. Even on our heightened security, I couldn't help but to admire just how beautiful she was.

"Where y'all at, over at General?" I asked Dollar-Sign, after securing my girl.

After he gave me confirmation, I hung up and made my way over to Oakland's General Hospital. I filled Tasha in on the way. Our dinner plans had to be postponed. Talk about understaffed and underpaid, Oakland's General Hospital saw on an average, eight-hundred-odd shooting victims a year. The city average for yearly homicides was a hundred and seventy-one. Oakland was a war zone and General was its *M*A*S*H* unit.

When we arrived on the scene, it was chaotic. Oakland PD was beating down a robbery suspect that had two bullet holes in his chest, who somehow got one arm free from the handcuffs.

I recognized one of the officer's they called Choaker, the leader of Oakland's corrupt police squad. The squad called themselves "The Riders" after the Oakland Raiders. We made brief eye contact, but I kept it moving. I needed to check up on my little brah.

Because Abel had been shot, I knew more members of *The Riders* would no doubt be lurking around his room, waiting to see who or what they'd pick up on.

Off in the distance a woman let out a soul piercing scream. Followed by a gut-wrenching wail. I couldn't help but to wonder if perhaps a mother had just lost another child to the street life. Shit, it is what it is. We lived and died by the sword.

Abel was loved by the Gas Nation Family and the waiting room outside the operating room showed it. My young killahs were out and from the looks on their young faces, they were ready for whatever.

"How's he doing?" I asked Dollar-Sign, who'd walked up and met me with a one-armed gangsta hug.

"Don't know. Ain't nobody came out dis bitch to tell us anything." A few soldiers came and stood by us. Most likely, trying to hear what we were discussing.

I looked over and noticed Kane standing in a corner by himself. He looked like the devil himself, ready to leave the gates of hell.

I had to focus though. I had to remain a general. I couldn't react like a common thug. I was a general with an army behind me. I turned toward Tasha and placed my hands on her shoulders like a parent would.

"Now listen, babe, I need you to be big mama. Stay here and talk to these fools to find out what's going on with little brah. Since this was a shoot-out, the police are fa'sho on their way and I got to get my soldiers out of here before we have our own version of Waco, Texas in Oakland.

"Call me if you have any problems or if you learn something." I handed her the keys to my car.

"Gas Nation! They fucked up and touched one of ours. Y'all already know that if it was any of you, Abe would be ready to turn up in a heartbeat. So, I want to burn this bitch down! Find Phoenix and burn everything he loves in the fucking process! Fuck Smack Mobb! Show these bitches what this Gas do!" That got them going! We stormed out of the emergency room like a second-half football team looking for redemption.

I followed behind Dollar-Sign. As I was walking through the doors, I caught Choaker's eyes watching me again. He was just beyond a window, openly staring at me.

Fuck'em!

*** 3X ***

De'Kari

.

CHAPTER 2

DOLLAR-SIGN

"In the beginning of this bloodline of mine/ I spark dis in a niggaz heart and cause him to shine/ Before all the rhyme lessons that I keep in my mind/ I owe you and I'll give my right hand to show you/ Whether it's fist or guns whatever it goes to/ It's me they go through if ever they want you/ I'd ignite that flame, that game been trynna scratch/ cain and gats and I'mma know just where my dogs are at/"

I didn't have to say it, DMX and the Ruff Riders were saying it for me. "This bitch ass nigga Phoenix must think this shit is a game, but I got something for his ass."

Since the faggot ass nigga wanna touch my blood, I'm fa'sho about to go H.A.M. *Hard as a Mothafucka.* When we shut one of his cook houses down, he should've known then this shit wasn't a game. That this Gas Nation was turned all the way the fuck up. I guess he didn't get the memo. But the nigga would today!

Word was, Phoenix was connected to a cat that was fucking with Gunz from the Neva Die Dragon Gang. I'm not even about to lie, them Neva Die Niggaz are the truth. Right now, they got the entire Bay Area in a chokehold on some *La Cosa Nostra* type shit. But I bow to no man. Not Ty Dollar-Sign.

The nigga Gunz just opened this all-in-one auto body, auto sales, car detailing and stereo installation shop, called The Koffee Shop in East Oakland over by 98th and Brookfield. That was our destination.

Tonight, niggaz would feel the wrath of Ty mothafuck'n Dollar-Sign.

"Them faggots trying to take down my people. I wanna see them splatter!" I yelled out, feeling like DMX.

19

We were five cars deep and we were bringing hell with us. Twenty niggaz in five cars, all with AR-15's. Yeah, we were about to act the fuck up!

"C1ty, I want you and C.J. to hit the back gate in exactly one minute." When I finished giving the directives, I popped a Molly in my mouth and chewed it up.

C1ty and C.J. were my cousins. As was Kane and Abel. They were family from San Francisco. So, this was a family affair.

The bitterness of the Molly made me choke a little, but the effects already had me on murder mode.

I had a baby AR-15 with a 150-round drum on my lap and To Da Left was in the passenger seat,

"Brah, you ready?" I asked To Da Left.

"Let's get it in," he replied.

I pulled up to the front of The Koffee Shop.

Scurrgggh! Scurrgggh! Tires screeched against asphalt as the other two vehicles followed in pursuit.

I threw the stolen Impala in park and hopped out. I was standing in front of the shop, looking like an Iraqi refugee, complete in green and black army fatigues.

Faaata! Faaaaaata! Taata! Taaat!

People inside scrambled in chaos, desperate for some type of cover from the big 223's spitting out our barrels.

Fiaaata! Fiaaata!

Taaata! Fiaaaata! Fiaaata!

For a while it felt like I was in the Army. Suddenly, over by the side of the building, a door opened.

Blaaaat! Blaaaat! Blaaaat!

Somebody was returning fire. Little Ducca took care of that problem. Once he aimed in that direction, the AR-15 did the rest. I enjoyed seeing the bodies drop. I didn't care who they were. Whether mechanic or mob nigga, anybody there was on the wrong side of the battlefield.

Period!

I saw what looked like a secretary desperately racing for cover and gunned her down too. I was past giving a fuck. Ty Dollar-Sign was out for blood.

"Arrgh!" Lil Gunna screamed out, signaling he had gotten hit. From the sound of the scream, it wasn't a bad shot. He would live.

By the time the firing pin clicked on empty, The Koffee Shop itself looked like it belonged in Iraq somewhere. There was quarter-size to golf-ball-size holes all over the building and what used to be brand new luxury cars. The ground was covered with so many shell casings, it looked like we were standing in a shooting gallery, instead of the empty parking lot of the shop. The acrid smell of sulfur was in the air.

And as for the bodies, Ty Dollar-Sign says fuck'em!

Careful not to let the tip of the barrel touch me, I opened the back door and tossed that bitch on the back seat. The barrel was so hot, I immediately smelled the seat burning. Next, I pulled my Glock .40 off my waist, in case any nigga decided he wanted to play hero. Then I jumped back into the driver's seat.

The sulfur from the gunpowder was starting to burn my lungs. I did a quick scan to make sure we didn't leave anyone behind and prepared to drive off. Lil Gunna was our only wounded.

Police sirens could be heard in the distance, but we would already be on Highway 880, headed north by the time they arrived. And if not, Ty Dollar had another 150-round drum, ready to wreak havoc on some shit.

First chance I got, I pulled my phone out and called Lil Ducca, who just happened to be a second cousin of mine as well.

"Talk to me, lil cousin, you good?" I was checking on Lil Gunna.

"Shit, this bitch'll be okay. He only got hit in the arm. But fuck that! Did you see me dancing with that thang?" *I sometimes forget Lil Ducca is only eighteen years old. These young niggaz be out here swinging these cannons, not thinking of the repercussions. They think this shit is really a game.*

"Yeah, you did yo *Dougie,* little nigga. Now, shut that shit up and get serious. Ditch that whip and take Blood to go see the old lady and get fixed up. We'll meet you back at the trap."

"No doubt, big cousin, I got you!"

I had family all over the Bay Area. My grandpa and grandma rooted down in Frisco before coming over the water to Oakland. But my uncles and aunts went all over this bitch.

C1ty and C.J. are from Double Rock. Ducca is from the Top Blythedale with Lil Bhudda and them. Kane and Abel are from the Bottom. Now the crazy part is, they all from the same hood in in San Francisco, but they all beefing. But Ty Dollar doesn't give two fucks about none of that. Out here, we're all family and that's all that matters.

*** 3X ***

Kane

When the Big Homie To Da Left made the call to take the gloves off and turn the heat up on Phoenix's bitch ass, I was more than ready. If he would've asked me, the moment we got the shipment of AR's from the Richmond nigga, we should've turned up. See, I'm not really a talkative person. Why should

I be? Most people didn't have shit worth listening to. Always gossiping and shit. The ones that did have something decent to say, always assumed because you were talking, that you were friends. I don't need friends, nor do I need to talk. A person could either respect my mind or respect my nine. Cause I sure as day will let that bitch talk for me. And she sings too!

Anyway, I found out a week ago where Phoenix's right-hand man stayed. I've just been sitting on that bit of information. I needed to see where the rest of my team's heads were at before I gave up the cake and ice cream.

Hell, once the gloves came off, it was party time for me. My little brother all laid up in a hospital bed full of bullet holes and these niggaz thought shit was real sweet. My nigga fighting for his life while this ratchet-mouth mothafucka is balls deep inside some mothafuck'n pussy! Niggaz must really got this Gas Nation fucked up!

This bitch ass nigga had the nerves to call himself *Shooter*. I don't know if he deserves the name or not. I just know after tonight he won't be shooting shit.

When I first walked in, he had his baby mama all bent over killing that dark, black ass. I didn't have the heart to stop him, so I pulled up a seat and watched with a wicked grin on my face. Enjoy it while you can, little nigga, enjoy it, I thought.

"That's right, bitch! Throw that shit at me. A nigga bout to nutt!" This cornball. See, he should've kept that shit to himself.

"Come on, Shoota! Ungh! Fuck me, daddy!" That bitch had to be faking that shit. This nigga was making more noise than his baby mama. He was making so much noise, he never heard me spark the lighter and put it to the tip of my Backwood, which I rolled while watching them.

Where the fuck is the security? Good question. I killed them already. Two niggaz were parked outside in a Buick Regal. They were more interested in the porno they were watching than being alive. As for the nigga in the living room, he opened the door to see why the headlights had come on in the car. He never got an answer. I killed him.

"Aargh shit! I'm cumming!" Nigga sounded like an old pirate, *Argh matey!*

"Now I could've come busting up in here and fucked your groove all up, Shooter, but I kept that shit 'G' and let you do yo *Dougie.* Now why don't you keep it 'G', turn around, shut the fuck up and tell Anika if she screams or yells, I'mma blow her head off. Oh! Try me!" I guess the cold steel sound of my voice got my point across.

"Look, man, I don't know who you is, but check this out. I got two hundred seventy-five thousand dollars in that black duffle bag in the closet. Gone and grab the dough and be about yo business." Oh! Okay, he wants to sound tough in front of the bitch.

A silenced 9mm bullet will shut that ass up. Pssst! I shot him in the leg to prove my point.

I guess I was wrong! From the way this nigga started screaming, my guess, this bitch ain't impressed.

"I don't like to waste my time or oxygen. I don't want your money, my nigga. I wanna give you an option. A, tell me what I came to find out and live. Or B, don't tell me, both of you die. Now, I don't have time for games, so choose."

"Fuck you mean, choose? Ain't no choice. He better tell you what the fuck you wanna know," Anika called out.

"What's it going to be, Shooter?"

"Man, how do I know you're telling the truth?" I shot him again, this time in the foot to let him know I was serious. He was so scared, he shit on the bed.

"Nigga, I told you I don't play games."

It took a moment for him to regain his composure from the gunshot. The entire time, Anika just sat there just shaking her head quietly.

"W-what you wanna know?" he asked, whimpering like a bitch.

How in the hell was this two-hundred-ninety-pound teddy bear anybody's second-in-command?

"Earlier today, niggaz rolled down on my brother, Abel. Shot him all up and killed his baby mama. Who made the play?"

He started laughing so hard, he farted. He was hysterical with laughter. I didn't know what was so funny until he spoke. Sweat was pouring down his face.

"Nigga, you that nigga, Kane? The nigga they call Death? Yeah, I shot your brother. You ole bitch-ass, wannabe ass nigga. Eat a dick! I hope your brother dies." He started laughing again, even more hysterically this time.

Psst! Psst! Psst! Psst!

I thought about blowing Anika too, but she had kept it too gangsta for me. I liked her get down.

With Shooter lying dead next to her on the bed, I walked over to the closet. Just like he said, there was a duffle of cash in the closet. I grabbed the bag and walked over to the bed and pulled out ten stacks, ten thousand, and dropped it on the bed next to her. I turned around and walked away.

Damn, she was a bad bitch! She still didn't flinch or make one sound. Not once did she beg for her life.

"Take me with you," she called out as I was walking through the bedroom door.

"What you say?" I didn't believe my ears. I was only seventeen. She was surely in her twenties and she had to know I was young.

"I love that gangsta shit and it's all throughout your body, lil daddy. I can see you are destined to be somebody and I wanna be with you." Here this bitch was butt-ass naked, sitting next to her dead baby daddy, who'd just finished fucking the dog shit out of her. And she had the audacity to come at me like that.

Fuck, this bitch was bad!

"Get dressed!" was all I told her.

She didn't hesitate either. While she got dressed, I put the stacks of money back inside the duffle.

"There are six more of them in the room next door and some dope," she told me while getting dressed.

I stood right where I was, looking dumbfounded. I was leaving this bitch with one-point-six million dollars all to herself, but instead of the money, she chose me.

Together, we walked into the other room. True, there were six more duffle bags. Five were cash, the sixth was dope. I couldn't help myself, we fucked right there on the floor inside the empty room.

*** 3X ***

CHAPTER 3

KANE

No, I didn't make her shower. I didn't give a fuck. I'm a little grimy nigga, so it's only right that my bitch is a little grimy too.

She walked up to me and reached for the duffle bag. Yeah, my heart sped up. So, what!

She took the duffle bag and dumped the money out on the floor. Next, she reached for my zipper and pulled my dick out. It was already fully hard. She was a dark-skinned cutie. Her chocolate skin covered my caramel color as she stroked me. The entire time she was looking in my eyes and licking her lips. Right there on top of a quarter of a million dollars, she dropped to her knees and started sucking my dick. I'm talking about that porn star, smile for the camera treatment. She was using a lot of hand action and even more spit. The slurping sounds were driving me crazy!

I pushed her head back, then made her turn around and bend over. Her big ole black ass was open and waiting.

"Mmm, come on, daddy. Give it to me good." After sucking on this dick, there was no way in hell she was going to ever call me lil daddy again.

Since she'd just finished fucking Shooter, Anika was nice and wet. I slid all eight inches deep inside of her. My eight inches of girth really opened her walls up. Once I felt her walls relax, I began pounding her pussy.

Slap! Slap!

Her fat ass jiggled as it smacked against my thighs.

"Ooh fuck! Oooh!" She was enjoying it, but I was only warming up. I could feel her fluids running out of her as I pumped.

Smack! Her ass looked too good, I had to slap it.

"Ungh! Ungh! Fuck me, Yes! Daddy, fuck this pussy hard!" As she moaned and got crazy, I couldn't help but think Shooter was a grown man, this is how he was supposed to hit that pussy.

Anika had shoulder-length hair that was flinging all over the place wildly. I grabbed a good handful of it and started giving her every single inch while I pulled her hair. All the way in and all the way out. Thrust after thrust. Hard, powerful strokes. She continued to love it.

"Daddy! Daddy! Yessss! Sssssh! Ooooh, daddy!"

Now she was throwing it back at me. I leaned forward and forced her face down inside the piles of money. This seemed to really make her go wild. Then I yanked her head back. "Bitch, who pussy is this? Whose?" I growled.

"Ungh...Oooh, it's yours, daddy! Yours, daddy!"

"Who?"

"Yours, daddy! This pussy belongs to Kane!" We both came together.

A little while later, my adrenaline kicked in, along with my common sense. Here I was in a house with four bodies surrounding it or in it, with over a million dollars in cash on me. It was time to get the fuck out of there. It took us two trips with me carrying two bags and her one, to get all the money out. Once loaded, we headed back to the trap.

*** 3X ***

JEFF TO DA LEFT

When Kane came walking into the trap, I was glad he was okay. It wasn't like him to miss anything, especially putting in work. But considering what he was dealing with regarding

Abel, I was being understanding. But when he walked in the door with Shooter's bitch, Anika, I didn't know what was up.

"Aaw, Brah! What the fuck she doing here?" Jeff said.

"You should blow that bitch head off."

Kane had to expect some of what he was hearing, if not more. He remained his silent self until C1ty spoke up.

"Nigga, if you brought that bitch here to run a train on her I'm fa'sho getting my dick sucked." That's when I heard Kane speak for the first time.

"Let everybody know and accept that bae is riding wit me. I'mma say it again, dis me. So, respect her like you would me. Now, everybody in here except her, knows I'm not with the talking shit. So please don't make me repeat myself. C1ty, take a couple of niggaz with you and grab them duffle bags out of my whip. To Da Left, those duffle bags are a gift from bae to me. I present them to the family, because we started this shit together," Kane said in a very stern voice.

When C1ty and the fellas came back, they were carrying all seven bags. I'd never in my life seen so much money before. At least, not in person. Maybe on TV or something. Or, okay, yeah at one of the cash houses. But what I mean is no one ever came and dropped one-point-six at my feet, like this nigga here!

I don't know what the next nigga would've done in a situation like that. I don't even know what a bitch-nigga would've done. I can only say what I did.

I called every member of Gas Nation to the trap and split the money evenly among every last one of us. First, I made sure to let it be known to everybody just how we came across the money.

Naturally, everybody was juiced, especially my young shooters. They'd never seen this amount of money themselves. I then took the duffle bag with all the dope and divided it amongst our trap houses. Even though Scarface was fucking with us on running the spots, it was still Gas Nation who handled the cash and the product. I mean, I didn't want niggaz to get tempted.

The more I reflected on the play Kane put down, the more impressed I became. It was some goon shit, but on a boss level. Nevertheless, celebrating wasn't about to bring an end to the war. So I made sure everybody knew to tighten up on security. I was sure that nigga Phoenix would try to come hard after this shit.

The following week were the funerals. We held a small private service for Mama J. on the same day the church gave an extremely long service for Reverend Jacobs.

I didn't know what I felt. I guess I was numb. The funeral brought back memories of Sheila that I had suppressed.

"Although we've come to the end of the road / Still I can't let go it's unnatural / you belong to me, I belong to you... oh!"

Boyz II Men sang it, but I felt it.

I know it was wrong, but I had feelings for Mama J. We'd been sleeping together for almost a year, plus she was a pivotal fixture in my life as far back as long as I could remember. That was two different types of love merged to form one bond.

Helping to kill her was one of the hardest things I'd ever done. But we live by the rules that we live by and we just try to make the right choices along the way, knowing that whatever these choices were, we understood we had to live by them.

Mama J. was truly the first person who'd ever cared for me. The first person to show me they cared, and I would forever miss her for that. For some reason though, it felt like I was betraying Jay by allowing myself to mourn for Mama J. I was betraying and disrespecting him by fucking his mama. Something had to be wrong with me.

I looked around the cemetery on 66th and MacArthur. All three of us, Ty Dollar-Sign, Tasha and me, had wet faces and heavy hearts, from what I could tell. They were probably going down memory lane like I was. Probably remembering the countless birthday parties we went to for Jay, or the time Mama J. played Santa Claus for the school play. These thoughts only made a nigga that much more lethargic.

"Shut up, you little bitch! Always crying and moping around like some sort of sissy." I couldn't see her, but I could hear her crystal clear. I looked around, trying to see where she was.

"Look at you! Look at you! I knew you'd grow to be a big punk and now look at you, sitting there crying like a bitch."

"Shut up, bitch! Shut up!" I jumped up and looked around the room again, but I didn't see her. Yet, I knew Sheila's voice when I heard it.

That bitch was still here!

*** 3X ***

TASHA

I know this is going to sound crazy, but they are not gone. Not Sheila, not Mama J. and certainly not Reverend Jacobs. I've always been able to see them. Almost like when Granny died, I could see and talk to Granny for years until Mama Carla got me to realize that Granny was indeed dead.

I've been seeing Jay since he was killed. I believed seeing him was a sign that he wanted us to avenge his death. However, we did that, and I could still see him standing over Mama J.'s casket, looking down on her. I didn't know it was possible for a ghost to cry. Yet there he was, crying his little heart out.

I wish I could talk to Jay. I miss him so much. I try to talk to him all the time, but he never responds.

"Shut up, bitch! Shut up!" Jeffrey made me jump out of my skin by hollering out and knocking his chair over as he stood up.

I felt a shock go through my body when I realized he was looking in Sheila's direction. I wondered if he could see her too. Did she do something to him?

Whoa! What if she spoke to him? Which would make sense him yelling shut up, if he could hear her.

I made my way over to my fiancé.

"Baby, what's the matter?" I asked while sliding my arms around him.

"That bitch, Sheila! She won't shut the fuck up!" He looked like he was on the verge of a nervous breakdown.

"Jeffrey, what do you mean she won't shut the fuck up? Sheila has been dead for years, daddy."

"I know she's dead, babe, but I can hear her inside my head." I wanted so bad to tell him she was standing right next to him. I didn't tell him because I didn't know how he would've looked at me if I told him I could see dead people. He would think I was crazy.

"Maybe her spirit is trying to tell you something." I suggested, though I highly doubted that shit.

"That bitch's spirit can suck my dick! That's all she could do for me." That ended Jeffrey's and my talk about Sheila.

The rest of the funeral, I watched while she whispered into his ear. Once, she looked my way mischievously before saying something to him. Jeffrey lifted his head and looked at me. Even though I knew I hadn't done anything wrong, I became nervous and he smiled at me and shook his head.

I spent the rest of the funeral observing everyone and everything. I wanted to know if the dead were bothering other people. Wondering if maybe, I wasn't the only one that could see them.

De'Kari

CHAPTER 4

TO DA LEFT

As I sat in Mama J.'s empty apartment, on the floor where the couch used to be, I reminisced on the times we shared right here in this living room.

I'm not even about to sit here and lie. Right now, I was not trying to be around anyone. I needed to try and get both my mind and emotions in order.

Lately, I haven't been me. I have been experiencing a lot of weird shit. Everything from hearing Sheila's voice constantly in my head, to always thinking about Mama J.

I know we did what we had to do, but a nigga was missing her like crazy.

A nigga can't go down memory lane in peace. That punk bitch Sheila is still in my head. She's making fun of me for killing the wrong people.

How could this stupid bitch claim to know who I've killed when she was already dead?

"You could never get things right, stupid! You and your little friends think that you're so smart. Ooops! But you killed the wrong ones. Ha-ha-ha-ha-ha." For days, she has been going on like this.

And if I said something to her, she would respond. I found that out the first day she started talking to me. The punk bitch hates when I ignore her.

"You never could get nothing right. A fucking moron is what you are, Jeffrey."

That's it! I've had enough of the stupid bitch. Her and her fucking mouth.

"Oh, yeah!" I yelled, the liquor slurring the two words. "I can't do nothing right, huh? Is that what you said? Well, apparently, I'm not too stupid. I killed you, didn't I, Sheeee-la! You and your crackhead friend."

I started thinking about the past.

The night Sheila died; I was walking through the darkened living room when a spark of a lighter startled me. Over on the broken-down filthy couch Sheila sat, butt-ass fuck'n naked, in all her natural horror.

The spark was from her cheap lighter as she sat smoking crack out of a glass stem. I mean fa'real, fa'real, this mothafucka was asshole butt naked, sweating like a Hebrew slave. Smoking in the middle of the living room like she lived by her motherfuck'n self or some shit. The foul stench of the sex was in the air. From where I was standing, it smelled like she hadn't showered for at least a month.

She'd done so many disrespectful things over the years, but this by far took the cake. How could a mother behave like this in front of a child? I just shook my head in disgust and started to walk away. I didn't need her to see the tears as they made their way down my face.

"Fuck you shaking your bitch ass head at me for, faggot? Mothafucka, this my house! And I'll do what the fuck I wanna do in my shit!" She sounded like an angry hyena as she roared at me.

"You could at least put some clothes on or do that inside your room." I was more hurt than anything. I couldn't believe she had so little respect for me, that she would allow me to see her like this.

"Bitch! Don't you come up in here with your little nappy-headed ass, thinking you can tell me what the fuck I can and cannot do in my own shit. I do what the fuck I wanna do in

my shit! It's your fault your father left in the first place. I should have flushed your little bitch ass down the toilet!"

Just then, I heard the toilet flush. A few minutes later, some nigga that resembled a Great Dane walking upright came out the bathroom.

"Bitch, what is you out here fussing about now?" It seemed the disrespect just wouldn't end that night as the Snoop Dogg lookalike came strutting out of the bathroom asshole butt naked.

When he saw me, he called out to Sheila, "Sheila, who's this little nappy-headed nigga?"

"Don't pay that little bitch no mind. He ain't nothing but a fucking mistake," she responded, just before putting the pipe back to her lips and taking a hit.

"Damn, little nigga, I thought my moms was a mean bitch," he chuckled as he walked past me.

Filled with rage, hurt and humiliation, I stormed down the hall to my bedroom. I would've slammed the door but that would've only let her know she'd gotten to me and I refused to give her that satisfaction.

I used that same resolve to hold back the tears begging to be released from my eyes. I hurriedly packed what I could into my old beat-up backpack and headed back out my room. I made it halfway down the hall before I remembered something. I rushed back in my room and grabbed my picture of Tasha off the dresser. On impulse, I snatched my brother's DMX CD out of the radio on my way out of the room the second time.

As I made my way down the hall, I silently wished I could make it out of the apartment without her saying one thing to me.

When I walked back into the living room, I got the shock of a lifetime. The skinny nigga was standing in front of Sheila, with his head tilted back. She sat her ass right there on the couch with her mouth filled with his dick.

I couldn't believe what the fuck I was seeing. I was more angered than disgusted. This was clear proof that she had no respect for me whatsoever or herself.

The sound of the nigga moaning and whimpering like a little bitch wasn't nearly as sickening as the sounds coming from her mouth. Just then, the nigga's head tilted down and he stared at me with the slimiest smile on his face. His yellow teeth and eyes made him look even more suitable for the role of Freddie Kruger in Nightmare On Elm Street. Just to egg me on and fuck with me even more, he looked down at Sheila and spoke.

"Ssss, yeah bitch, suck that big black dick." To my added horror, she began moving her head back and forth with impossible speed. I was frozen, paralyzed by shock.

The slurping sounds she was making were horrid. The entire ordeal only lasted a few moments before I was able to break my paralysis. At this exact moment, Sheila in my eyes, stopped being my mother.

My blood was boiling. How could this bitch play me like that? I'd put up with my share of shit over the years, but this surely took the cake. Never again! I was done. My mind was made up. Tonight, this bitch was going to learn about treating me the way she does.

I made my way back down the hallway to my room, while devising on a plan to kill Sheila and her lover. As the sound of their lovemaking echoed throughout the apartment, I racked my brain, thinking of the best way possible to carry out my objective.

Sheila didn't have any respect. She was moaning and screaming at the top of her lungs. As if that wasn't enough, the broken couch continuously slammed against the wall. Over and over again.

I waited patiently in fury. Knowing I would get my reward for putting up with her bullshit just a little while longer, I came up with a simple plan.

Sheila always kept a can of gasoline so she could dip cotton in it and use the cotton ball as a lighter.

I waited for a full forty-something minutes after they were done having sex before I made a move. I went to Sheila's room, where I knew she would be.

I could hear the loud sounds of their snoring coming down the hall. It sounded like Sheila and the Freddy-Kruger-looking mothafucka were having a verbal battle inside the room over who could snore the loudest.

I opened the door to Sheila's room, and it looked like Hurricane Katrina and Hurricane Andrew both hit her room at the same time, shit was everywhere. The stench in the room was so strong, I would not have been surprised if there were two or three dead bodies in the room.

I stood at the door, scanning the mess looking for the can. I finally found it sitting in the corner. After climbing over every form of trash imaginable, making sure not to wake them up, I retrieved the gas can and poured it all over the trash inside the room. Next, I trailed a line of gasoline as I exited the room.

I made sure to close the door behind me, but not before taking one last pitiful look at Sheila's naked form laying across the filthy bed. After closing the door, I poured more gasoline on the floor just outside the door.

For a moment, I hesitated. Then the image of her sucking his dick flooded my memory and I struck a match and dropped it on the floor. With the two of them trapped asleep in the room, there was no way they would escape the fire.

As I left the apartment, I was oblivious to everything around me. The piss smell in the hallways, the night air, the sounds of the nightlife, none of that registered in my head as I walked through the projects.

Somehow, I ended up at Jay's apartment. When Ms. Johnson opened the door, I guess she could see it clearly written on my face that something was wrong.

"Aww, you poor baby, come here." The moment I felt her warm secure embrace, my resolve finally broke down and the tears flowed. Ms. Johnson was used to me going home, only to come back because Sheila would lock me out of the house, or some other form of abuse.

I was at Mama J.'s old apartment to gather all my shit. After spending time thinking about the past, I grabbed my stuff and made my way back to my Tahoe. Once I started it up, I immediately pressed play on 3X Krazy. That was on my playlist.

As I was pulling off, I was busy fumbling around in the ashtray looking for the half a blunt I had placed there. I never saw it coming, bending down to look in the ashtray saved my life.

BOOM!

The sound of a 12-gauge shotgun woke the night up. The blast blew the driver's side window out and glass rained down my body.

The Glock on my lap materialized in the palm of my hand.

BOCCA! BOCCA! BOCCA!

The nigga standing outside my door got hit in the head and the chest. He got caught slipping cause he wasn't ready for the recoil when he pulled the trigger. His 12-gauge kicked when he shot it, knocking him in the head, momentarily dazing him.

I wasn't safe yet.

Scurrrrrrrrr!

An all-black O.J. Simpson Bronco came skidding to a stop in front of me, blocking my path. When all four doors opened up, I got lightweight spooked. Every last nigga that stepped out was holding a choppa. I didn't have to think. I dove as far into the back as I could. My AR-15 was on the second-row seat. I landed on the third.

"What's up wit Blood?" someone called out. I was confused, because that was a Gas Nation saying.

Taata! Taata! Taata! Taata!

Taaata! Taata! Taata! Taata!

"Gas Nation, bitch!" It was C1ty and C.J. They were my security for the night because Kane was at the hospital with his brother. They opened fire first, but the niggaz in the Bronco returned fire with equal power. It gave me the time to grab my shit.

Taataa! Tataaa! Tataa!

The driver and the nigga next to him did the Harlem Shake as my AR played music. My adrenaline was pumping so hard, I did some Denzel Washington, *Man On Fire* type shit. I marched in their direction in the middle of the street, like I didn't have a care in the world.

C1ty and C.J. took care of the other two niggaz. I heard a vehicle approaching the moment all the shooting ceased. I didn't take any chances, I spun around and let that bitch have it. My boys did too.

As soon as we finished, the three of us jumped in our vehicles and got the fuck out of dodge.

Gas Nation, bitch!

*** **3X** ***

De'Kari

CHAPTER 5

DOLLAR-SIGN

"See, that is exactly what the fuck I am talking about! This faggot ass nigga Phoenix think shit is sweet over here. We got to dead that nigga, man. Straight up, and stop playing games with him." Hearing To Da Left tell me what the fuck happened to him in Acorns had me extremely pissed off.

First, it was Abel getting hit and being in the hospital, now this. Fuck all this dumb shit, it was time to let this nigga Phoenix know once and for all exactly who the fuck he is dealing with.

I made eye contact with every person in the room. These niggaz needed to know just how serious I was. If the sweat on my forehead or my turnt-up level didn't tell them, fa'sho my eyes would. I locked eyes with Kane for a moment. I'm sure it went unnoticed, but my words wouldn't.

"Kane, you are my mother's sister's son. I love you like a brother, but I still have to ask you. Have you tried to get info out of your girl, considering she was rocking with Phoenix's top dawg?" Now wasn't the time to worry about niggaz emotions. Now was the time to make mothafuck'n moves.

That nigga just stared at me for so long, I thought he wasn't going to answer. Family or not, I was willing to fuck the little nigga up to make an example to everybody, if I had to.

When he finally spoke, his voice was low and calm, but it dripped with venom and death.

"First and foremost, don't be questioning me about my bitch, that's my job. If she knew something, she would've already told me. As for that nigga, you can consider him dead. I got tired of watching you niggaz play 'Black Ops' with his ass. So, I called a play. That bitch ass nigga will be dead before the end of the week. As long as my brother is laid in the hospital, '*Anybody Can Get It!*'" That's how Kane was, blunt and to the point.

Abel made it out of the Intensive Care Unit, but the doctor said he had a long way to the road of recovery. Apparently, he had been shot ten mothafuck'n times. Two arteries were nicked, which almost killed him. Another bullet punctured his right lung, which collapsed twice. He had some more shit wrong with him, but I blocked that shit out.

"My nigga, you over there acting like you the only nigga that want a piece of this nigga Phoenix, or the only nigga whose gun bust. Nigga, I stay on my Pistol Pete." I had to let him know.

Kane stood up like he was ready to get it poppin.

"Naw, y'all hold the fuck up!" It was To Da Left speaking up for the first time in this meeting.

"What we ain't about to do is let mothafuckas get us to be at each other's throat like rabid animals. Phoenix and his team are the objectives. I really want to take him out myself, but at the end of the day, I don't care who kills that nigga as long as it's a member of Gas Nation. Kane, I know you can handle yourself, so carry out the play you called. If you need any support, you know that Nation got you," To Da Left continued.

"Dollar-Sign, I need you to focus on this money and the couple of big moves we have lined up. Now, a nigga ain't questioning yo gangsta, but we all got positions to play. My nigga, I need you to get us back on track. The last couple of months has cost us financially and we need to bounce back.

"Now, I got the meeting with Booker about the new shipment of guns and some other shit he wants to drop on a nigga'z lap. C1ty, you and C.J. stay on my six again." He turned back in my direction and asked, "Is that cool?"

"Off the top, brah, you already know me. I'm about Gas Nation. Speaking of which, you know Juneteenth is coming up. Given the amount of blood the streets have been seeing, I think we should do something big." I threw it out there.

"What do you have in mind?" To Da Left asked.

"Nigga, let's throw a block party! No, let's do a hood party! That would be wild," C.J. called out.

"What the fuck is a hood party?" I asked.

"It's a block party, but..." He stood up and got animated. "Say we shut down the projects and turn it to one big party field. Then, we shut down all the traffic on that block. All of Acorn will be one big party and the whole hood is invited." C.J. painted a vivid picture in all of our minds.

"Then that's what we're doing," I said.

"We have to make sure this Phoenix situation is really over before we do this. I'm not trying to endanger all these little kids and shit." This time To Da Left was looking at Kane when he spoke.

In response, Kane just nodded his head up and down.

"Yo, boss, it's about that time," J-Roc walked into the room and informed me.

I checked my watch and realized he was right. I walked in the back room and retrieved the four duffle bags, which J-Roc helped me carry and we made our exit.

I was meeting up with Scarface and a few other homies to drop some work on them. Shit was good for the Nation as far as the drug shit went. We were buying grade A-1 pure dope at wholesale prices, throwing our four points per brick and flying these bitches across the pavement.

Not only that, but we still had our trap houses where we broke down each brick into dime rocks. We were killing them. Now that we were straight with the coke, I was trying to open up some avenues with the heroin, fentanyl and crystal meth.

Fentanyl was the new synthetic heroin, and meth was the new synthetic crack and crank. All of it was cheap and it was the future.

Inside each duffle bag, there were ten kilos. I dropped them off to their prospective locations, saving Scarface for last. As a way of saying thank you for the support he and his homies gave us in the war against Phoenix, Jeff To Da Left decided to give them their own trap off of Cypress Street. On top of which, five of the kilos in the duffle bag were for him on G.P.

"Okay, so we gonna get it like this every Thursday and in turn, I will be ready for you the following day with your bread? Right?" Scarface was repeating the deal we worked out.

"Bet that. Never keep the money and bread together. Plus, I always like to pick up the money a day later. Because it gives you another full day to trap and make sure everything is straight. That's an extra day to make sure your count is right and so is my money."

"No doubt, Homie. Me and my people always make sure we do good business. It's the only way we know how to do business. Feel me?" He looked like he took offense to my last statement.

Shit, he'd get over that shit real fast. There wasn't room for emotion in this game. A nigga had to shoot straight from the hip. You could respect it or check it. After getting an understanding with Scarface, a nigga was feeling hungry. When I mentioned it to J-Roc, he let me know he was hungry too.

I had a taste for something different, so I decided to head over to the east and hit up Everett and Jones. It's the best barbeque joint in the Bay area. We made the drive from the west to the east, knocking 3X Krazy's *Stacking Chips* album. When we pulled up, the restaurant didn't look too busy. That was cool with me because I was trying to get in and out. I hated East Oakland with a passion. To me, the only thing good in it was the food spots.

Inside, only a couple of people were either waiting on orders or placing orders. We waited five minutes to place our orders and another twenty before it came. The entire time we waited, the smells coming from out the kitchen kept reminding a nigga of how hungry he was.

Just as a nigga was grabbing our food, I heard the front door open. Even though I didn't know the two niggaz that walked in, the hairs on the back of my neck stood up.

Then it happened. J-Roc came off the hip with both 38's. I reached for my waist for my .44 Magnum and spun around at the same time. I came face-to-face with Phoenix.

His goons had their guns out, trained on J-Roc and me.

"You know what time it is, nigga! Bust the move!" I challenged him.

This crazy old mothafucka laughed at me.

"If I wanted you dead, youngsta, you would have been dead." He snapped his finger and all of his goons lowered their guns. "But now, youngsta, we need to talk because this shit is getting out of hand."

"What the fuck you come to me for? I don't do the talking." Everyone knows I don't have the temper for politics.

"Exactly. I come to you because you're the hot head. If I can reason with you, I don't need to worry about everyone else. Had I spoken to Jeff To Da Left, I'd still have to worry about you. Coming to you first, I'm killing two birds with one stone, per se and making sure the situation is taken care of." His logic made sense, but I still wasn't convinced.

"Nigga, do you think I'm stupid enough to fall for some shit like that?" I asked him.

"Take a look behind you, youngsta."

When I did, I noticed two things. The chick that was handing me my food had a 9mm in her hands, instead of my bags. Standing next to her was the second thing I noticed. Three niggaz had come in through some back door. All had cannons on us. If shit got ugly, there was no way in hell J-Roc and I would make it out alive.

I looked over at J-Roc. The look on his face said if I gave the order, he'd die airing this bitch out. I'mma gangsta to the full extent of the word, but I ain't no dummy.

If this old crazy mothafucka wanted to talk, then I would at least hear him out before we *Call of Duty* this bitch.

I gave J-Roc the sign to lower his cannons.

"Looks like you got the upper hand, fa'sho. Might as well hear you out. Ain't like I got a mothafuck'n chance anyway."

He smiled and motioned to a table. "Have a seat."

When we sat down, I sat and waited for him to speak. I mean, after all, it was his show.

"I'm going to be blunt with you, simply because it is the only way you will respect it. I don't know why Gas Nation declared war on me. Up until now, I didn't take you seriously. Have I responded to any of your attacks? No, but if y'all don't fall back, I will annihilate all of you," he said as a matter of fact.

"Fuck you mean, nigga? You sent yo niggaz to our trap. Tried to knock me and To Da Left down after I killed that faggot ass nigga, Ugz," I spit with fire.

"Why in the hell would I go to war with a bunch of youngstas over a snitch? Yeah, Ugz was my cousin and I loved that nigga to death. But he was a rat. I chalked up whatever happened to him as the game. God dealing with his ass. I never sent anyone at you or at your team, for any reason. Now, I came close to lighting that ass up when y'all blew up my cook shack. However, y'all did a favor on that one, so I didn't release my kill squad." Just then, two plates of food arrived and were placed in front of us. A bag with everything we had ordered was given to J-Roc, who was standing to my right with his back against the wall.

While Phoenix took the time to eat some of his food, I asked him, "If what you're saying is true, then who is getting at my team?"

He took a big bite of one of the sausages on his plate and replied, "Your guess is as good as mine on that one, youngsta. I was curious myself, so I shot a few arrows to see just where they would land. Problem is, they never landed anywhere. All I can tell you is, in coming for me, you're making an enemy out of a pretty lucrative potential ally." Phoenix spent another twenty-some-odd minutes convincing me that he wasn't behind the attacks on us.

When I told him Shooter had taken responsibility for what had happened to Abel, Phoenix said he would have done the same thing, had I been trying to bitch him in front of his old lady. I had to admit, I would have also.

It took some convincing, but an hour after walking into Everett and Jones, I walked out believing we had been wrong all along. Phoenix wasn't that nigga we were at war with. The question was, if he wasn't the enemy, then who was?

*** **3X** ***

De'Kari

CHAPTER 6

KANE

If someone were to ask me, I'd tell them Dollar-Sign is getting soft. How the fuck he gonna say he made a deal with that bitch ass nigga Phoenix all by his self? Telling us he believed the bitch ass story the nigga fed him.

Nigga, fuck that!

My brother was laid up in Highland Hospital fighting for his life and this nigga talking about holding hands and singing "Kumbaya" with the mothafuckas that put him there.

Where the fuck they do that at?

In all black from head to toe, I opened the door and made my move. Creeping in the shadows, I came up to the first lookout. With a long blade knife I picked up from the Army Surplus Store, I slit his throat. As he fell, I caught his body and laid it down softly so it wouldn't make any noise. I jumped the gate to the backyard and waited in silence for the sound of a dog or anything else. Nothing came.

As I climbed the back steps, my heart thumped in my chest. The adrenaline raced through my veins. I was ready for anything.

I listened with my ear to the door for what seemed a lifetime, trying to find any sound of life whatsoever.

I pulled out my lock picking kit and within minutes, I was closing the back door behind me. Once it was closed, I waited another lifetime, but no one came. No sound emitted from anywhere in the house.

I pulled my Desert Eagle out and began to make my way through the house. When I heard the bed squeaking and the sound of a bitch moaning, I figured this was too easy.

The rest of the house turned up empty. I checked it first so no one could pop up behind me. I got to the door where the sounds of fucking were coming from. Sure enough, they were getting it in. The bitch was sounding like he was killing her shit.

I opened the door slowly. The squeakiness of the hinges were masked by the sounds of loud screams and her cries of passion.

I raised my arm, then took aim.

Click-Clack

KABOOOM!

I never saw the trap door in the floor swing open or the 12-gauge shotgun that hit me in the chest. The blast sent me airborne, crashing into the wall behind me. The pain was too intense.

"Kane, I knew you would still come for me regardless of what I told Ty Dollar-Sign." Through the pain, I could see Phoenix walking towards me.

"The problem is, you should have listened, because I told him the truth. I'm not responsible for the attack on your brother or anyone on your team. But you came into my domain. You violated my space. I don't have a choice but to kill you." For the first time, I noticed the cannon in his hand.

My stomach and chest felt like a thousand holes were burning in them from the shotgun blast. I couldn't feel my left arm.

He closed the gap and stood over me.

BOOM! BOOM! BOOM! BOOM!

I didn't realize the Desert Eagle was still in my hand until I raised it, purely out of instinct. I continued squeezing.

I was slow getting up but when I did, I turned towards his wife.

BOOM! BOOM! BOOM!

I fed that bitch with no hesitation. I reloaded and returned fire back on Phoenix. All face shots. I wasn't going to make the mistake he made.

BOOM! BOOM! BOOM!

When the 12-gauge hit me, it was in the chest. Although the force of the blow sent me airborne and broke a few ribs, my bulletproof vest saved my life. Vest or not, Phoenix wouldn't survive my head shots.

Like I told 'em, I was done playing Black Ops with this nigga. When my bitch told me she could get the address to where this nigga Phoenix laid his head, I knew then it was only a matter of time before I knocked his noodle out his shit.

*** 3X ***

To Da Left

To say I was pissed off when I learned that Kane killed Phoenix would be an understatement. I was fucking furious! Not only because I was going off Dollar-Sign's instinct, which told him Phoenix had been telling the truth. Also, because I made it perfectly clear we'd investigate Phoenix's claim.

I couldn't focus on that shit though. Natalia, that little Russian mixed with black chick, hit me up about cashing in on our debt to her.

Back when our sole purpose was finding out who killed Jay, it was Natalia that alerted us to Uncle Bernard and his fucked-up, sordid tales of sexual torture. A tale that would ultimately end in his death, at the hands of Dollar-Sign and myself. As well as Mama J's death by all three of us, Dollar-Sign, Tasha and me.

Damn! Mama J., why did you just have to pop up in a nigga'z head like that? You already know a nigga misses you like fuck. I wish I could hear Mama J.'s voice instead of that bitch, Sheila's. But that would be too much like right.

I pulled in the front of the address Natalia gave me. My two shooters, C.J. and C1ty, were in the passenger seat and backseat ready to go at the slightest weird shit.

I don't know why dudes be having their security drive them around and shit. It didn't make sense to me. If this nigga's job is to shoot, how is he going to do that driving? Nigga, I will drive, you shoot, straight up.

The address turned out to be a small bar called Smirnoff, of all things. We walked into the joint like we walked into any other joint. Like we owned it!

The lights were dim, but I could still see enough to tell it was the type of bar whose patrons were filthy rich. I'm talking about plush carpeting, booths with butter soft leather on the seats.

Behind the bar that looked like it was made out of expensive German oak, was only top-shelf liquor. Real talk. The smoke didn't choke the air out of you. It was smooth. I knew it had to be expensive cigars, especially since the smoke had a sweet underline to it.

I don't know if I can call him a host, but somebody appeared and escorted us to a booth in the back. Seconds later, she appeared. Natalia slid into the booth across from me. C1ty was in the booth across from us, C.J. was in the booth in front of us.

"Jeffrey, it is good to see you." I swear to God, her voice sounds like someone playing a harp.

"It's good to see you again as well. But I thought I asked that you call me Jeff or To Da Left? Jeffrey sounds just too formal."

"Ok, Jeff, my apologies. I see you boys have been very busy."

The dude that showed us our seats came over and said something in Russian.

"Would you gentlemen care for anything to drink?" Natalia asked.

"I'll have a double shot of Don Julio 1942. Nothing for the fellas. They don't drink on the job," I answered.

Natalia spoke in Russian and he left. Then she brought her attention to me and spoke.

"I waited for you and Ty to settle your affairs as I promised. Now it's time for you guys to honor our arrangement. I have a few things I need tidied up in Russia. Shouldn't take more than a month for the two of you."

I was wondering just how she knew about Kane and Phoenix. I was going to ask, but decided against it.

"First things first. I'm not about to have my life and my brother's solely in your hands halfway around the world, it will be four or five of us coming. Second, I need a good bank overseas that won't ask many questions, so I won't run into any expense problems. I am also going to need you to set up a meeting with an arms dealer. That is the first thing of the utmost importance."

She chuckled. Just when I was about to get in her ass, o'boi came back with our drinks. When he left, she beat me to the punch.

"Jeff, you won't be needing a bank nor an arms dealer. I assure you all of your expenses will be taken care of. Regardless of what they are. As for weapons, just tell me what you need, and I will supply them. You'll be flying on my private jet, so you can bring your personal weapons. But if you told me you need a tank with twelve surface-to-air missiles, they would be waiting for you as soon as we land.

"The only thing I need for you to worry about is the assignments themselves. As for how many of you come, I'll leave the decision totally up to you. My guys can't be used because I can't afford any of it to be linked back to me." I can't lie, I was wondering how her little Russian pussy might taste.

The bitch Sheila used right then to start talking shit.

"Fucking faggot. You wouldn't know what to do with a good girl like her. You fucking pencil dick. It's okay, you're going to get yours. I promised you this." I ignored her ass like I'd been doing for the past couple of weeks.

"So, when is your jet going to be fueled and ready to go?" I asked. The sooner we got this shit over with the better for all of us.

I already made my mind up. C.J. and C1ty were coming with us. I wanted Kane to come as well but didn't know if he would stay with Abel in the hospital.

On second thought, maybe it would be good to leave Kane if Phoenix was telling the truth. This way we still had somebody competent enough to lead our soldiers if something was to pop off.

"We'll be taken off from hangar A-1 at ten-forty-five tonight. Your names will be given to security with specific instructions that you are bringing guests. The number will not be specified. This will get you onto the airfield with no problem." Natalia laid it all out for me.

Once our little meeting was over, C1ty, C.J. and I left with the intentions of seeing her again in a few hours.

*** 3X ***

CHAPTER 7

DOLLAR-SIGN

I don't give a fuck how ghetto a mothafucka thought I was, a nigga was about to board a jet. I felt like a made mothafuck'n man. So, I knew I had to stunt!

I was knocking that old G-Unit "Stunt 101" as I pulled the big body Benz through the security gate. I was feeling like 50-Cent as the VS Diamonds on a nigga glistened.

Young To Da Left was in the passenger seat with our wolves behind us in all-black Dodge Durango. After making it through the checkpoint with no hassle, we followed the instructions given by security until we found the appropriate hangar.

Natalia was already waiting for us. Lil mama was super bad with a capital S. I am not the type to mix business with pleasure, so I admired her from afar.

"I am glad you could make it, gentlemen," She called out as we pulled inside the hangar and got out of the vehicles.

"I bet this is gonna end up being one trip that a nigga don't wanna miss," I responded.

"Oh, I can guarantee you it's going to be a trip you will always remember," she shot back at me and smiled.

"That's one way of looking at it. Another could be, I don't think we had a choice in the matter," To Da Left said as he walked around the Benz to give Natalia a hug.

That nigga said that shit jokingly. But we all knew that shit was the truth, with an underlying hint of only God knew what.

The plane itself looked like a small apartment. A small, phat-ass apartment. Everything from butter soft Italian leather down to cherry wood cabinets. Two servers ensured us whatever we wanted, they would provide, from expensive drinks to steak.

She even had two closets full of different kinds of fur coats and triple goose-down feather coats for us to wear. The jackets were in almost every size a man can wear.

When the flight attendant came through, I ordered a glass of Louis the 13th and a nice filet mignon dinner. Like I said, I was feeling like 50 Cent and I was stuntin.

The flight to Russia took twelve hours. The last hour and a half, To Da Left, Natalia and I used the time to go over the shit she wanted us to do. The shit didn't seem that bad to me. She wanted us to kill some old white mothafuckas. Fa'sho, that wouldn't be hard.

We landed in Moscow and all I could think was, *Thank God this bitch had fur coats for niggaz, cause it was fucking freezing.* Snow was piled up high as shit, while fresh snow was falling like we landed in a fucking blizzard.

Some of her men were already waiting for us in three SUV's. Natalia, To Da Left and I hopped in the second one. C1ty and C.J. jumped in the third one. The duffle bag that had our arsenal was sitting right on my lap. Shit we'd just flown all the fuck across the world to some foreign land. I wasn't about to get caught out of pocket. Therefore, the duffle bag was not about to leave out of my sight for nobody.

She had just set us up in a suite at the Ritz-Carlton. Fresh off the jet, we went directly to the suite. All I'm going to say is I'm beginning to think I could get comfortable with this way of living. Very comfortable.

*** 3X ***
To Da Left

The suite she got us was beyond boss shyt! It came with three rooms, four and a half bathrooms, two living rooms and a sitting area. There were so many TV's in the suite, I could have opened a flat screen TV appliance store. The furniture was made from names I didn't know and couldn't pronounce. Dollar-Sign and I had our own rooms, while C1ty and C.J. shared the last one. At least that was the plan, until C.J. decided to sleep in one of the living rooms.

I wasn't into wasting time, so our first target we decided to deal with that night. But, for the moment, a quick nap would be nice. I took a piping hot shower and relaxed my muscles before climbing into bed and drifting off.

A few hours later, I woke up from my nap feeling like a million dollars and ready to put in some work. Our target was supposed to be a frequent guest at the Madriaan Bar. It was supposedly a small cozy joint with brick walls and wooden tables.

The problem was large windows that faced the street. Which meant passersby could look in and see some shit they shouldn't see. But I'd take care of that problem when the time came.

The plan was for me and Dollar-Sign to go in and do duties, while C1ty and C.J. watched our backs. There was never a need for every gun to go inside. The smart thing was always to leave somebody covering your rear which guaranteed you wouldn't run into any surprises on your way out.

The thing that didn't sit well with me was us having to use her guys as drivers. But let's face it, we had no other choice. We didn't know enough to be able to navigate our way through the streets. If something went wrong, it would put us in a fucked-up position. We needed someone who could get us out of there in case the police showed up or if reinforcements came.

A knock came at the door while I was in my thoughts, signaling it was time to go.

We drove for what seemed like forever down side streets, making twists and turns. I knew if we got separated from her men, I had no doubt in my mind we would not make it back. When I looked at Dollar-Sign, the look on his face told me he was thinking the same thing.

Guess we better not fuck up!

The driver pulled over and said something in Russian, while pointing at a building. I figured he was saying the building was Madriaan Bar. I made eye contact with Dollar-Sign and together, we stepped out of the SUV.

The cold night air slapped us ferociously in the face. The big thick fur coat not only helped keep us warm, but they also concealed our weapons. I was carrying two 9mm, both with 50-clips on them. Dollar-Sign had a baby AR with him, hidden underneath his coat.

The snow was falling so much, I could barely make out the building the driver pointed at.

"C1ty, I want you to post up right here and make sure these mothafuckas don't try to leave us or pull any other funny shit," I told little brah as I assessed the situation.

"I got you, brah."

"C.J., you post on the sidewalk by the door, while me and brah do our *Dougie*. If it doesn't look right, then burn it the fuck down."

"Got it, brah," he responded.

The three of us walked across the street.

Our target was an older, fat white guy. He was supposed to be seated at a table with a couple blonde girls. It should be a simple in and out.

"You ready?" I asked Dollar-Sign.

His response was simply, "Gas Nation."

I pulled my Donald Trump mask over my face and followed Dollar-Sign in his George H. Bush mask into the bar. Simplicity went out the window the moment we saw all the guests. There were about twenty to thirty guests in total. However, every booth had an older fat white man sitting at it with some blondes.

What were we going to do? Failure was not an option. With that thought in mind, I looked over at Dollar-Sign. He simply shrugged his shoulders, like fuck it!

Boc! Boc! Boc! Taata! Taata! Taata! Boc! Boc! Boc! Taata! Taata! Taata! Boc! Boc! Boc!

We pulled our weapons and knocked down everybody in the building. Bodies were dropping, while others scrambled to get out the way of the 223's. It was useless though, because the 9mm's bullets were flying everywhere the 223's missed. It was a massacre, but a hell of a way to make a statement.

Almost a minute later, Dollar-Sign and I were making our way across the street with C1ty back to the SUV.

Once we were all safely inside, the driver simply smiled and pulled off.

*** **3X** ***

The weight of the Ruger P-89 equipped with a silencer made me feel somewhat secure in the foreign hallway as I was walking, but my heart was racing a million miles a minute. Someone would have thought this was my first drill mission. Truth be told, I was informed our next target would be a state diplomat and that shit had me nervous as fuck.

The house was quiet. It smelled like expensive oak and cigars. I was in Moscow's equivalent to a governor's mansion.

I followed the hall until it reached the desired bedroom. I tried the knob and the door opened with ease. Silently, I stepped into the room, only to find it empty. Looking around, I noticed a light coming from underneath the bathroom door. Gun in hand, I made my way over to the door. When I put my ear up to the door, I could barely make out what sounded like paper. I grabbed the doorknob and yanked it open.

My target was sitting on the toilet reading the newspaper. He looked up at me frozen in fear from the sight of the gun in my hand.

"Tell me, does she have something hanging over you too?" he asked in perfect English once the initial shock wore off.

"Nah, this is more or less a favor for a favor," I told him before pulling the trigger.

His head exploded into a cloud of pinkish-gray spray all over the wall behind him.

I turned to exit the house.

3X

CHAPTER 8

TO DA LEFT

"You guys have done a wonderful job thus far. In fact, you've done such a good job that our third target has gotten a last moment of change of heart, regarding his opinion on who should run this family. I guess he sees I am just as vicious as my father, if not as vicious, even more so." Natalia was seated behind her desk as we spoke.

We were in her office at the back of the night club she owned. A popping ass nightclub at that.

"So, what does that have to do with our arrangement?" Fuck the good news I wanted to hear the bad shit. So, I could prepare for it and mow through it.

"It means you're going home sooner than previously arranged. In fact, I called you guys here to show you my appreciation for your help. The night is on me. I want you guys to relax and enjoy yourselves. I assure you, there isn't a thing you could want, that I couldn't get for you. All you have to do is ask." She spoke out in Russian and one of her grizzly bear security guards opened the door and stepped out.

When he stepped back in, he was followed by a string of some of the baddest white bitches I had ever laid my eyes on.

"Boys, these are some of the best girls in all of Mother Russia and they have been instructed to meet your every demand. Enjoy!"

My team looked at me hungrily waiting for my approval, which I gave to them when I nodded my head. Why shouldn't they enjoy themselves? They've been working hard and deserved some fun. But that shit wasn't for me. Not only did I have a queen holding me down, I only messed with sistahs. No matter how good they looked, they were not my flavor.

One by one, they left out of the office with one or two women on their arms and a huge smile on their face. A couple of girls tried to get my attention. I politely declined their offers.

When everyone had left out of the office except for Natalia and me, she turned to me and asked, "Why aren't you having fun with the girls?" she asked me like I just did the dumbest shit in the world.

"I'm not trying to disrespect your hospitality or anything by refusing your gifts. It's just that my heart belongs to someone. Whether in Oakland or in Russia, I'mma hold her down just like I know she'll hold me down," I told her as I sat down in one of the plush chairs across from her desk. "But what I will take is some of that exclusive vodka I know you got on deck."

She let out a laugh. "Oh, so you just know I got something like that, huh?"

"If you don't, you're not Russian. I hear all real Russians drink only the good stuff," I joked with her.

Natalia stood up and walked her sexy self across her office to her personal bar and opened the fridge. She retrieved a bottle and two small glasses and made her way over back to the desk and sat down.

"Mr. Watkins, you want the best. Well, this is the best that Mother Russia has to offer." She told me as she cracked the bottle and filled the two glasses about three fingers high and handed me one.

It was like something I never experienced before. The burn was minimal, yet the bite was out of this world. Similar to the ways of Don Julio 1942, but better. I looked for the name on the bottle, it was Russo-Baltique Vodka.

"Now I must say, that is some good shit. How much does a bottle like this go for?" Right when I asked the question, my cell phone started ringing.

Seeing that it was my baby, I didn't hesitate to answer it, first asking Natalia to excuse me while holding up my index finger.

"What's up, babe?"

Her speech was rapid and filled with animation, barely understandable to the naked ear. But I got her message loud and clear. After calming her down, I instructed her to go straight home. It was then that she told me she was already home. I told her I would have someone at the house in less than ten minutes.

After promising Tasha I was on the next thing smok'n back home, I looked at Natalia and told her, "We have to go now."

"What's wrong?" she asked, picking up the phone, punching some numbers.

"Someone just tried to kill my queen." Those were my only words.

*** 3X ***

De'Kari

CHAPTER 9

TASHA

I decided to make today an honorary day, "Me-Day." A day full of pampering and spoiling "Me." I started off by going to Massage Envy, where I had the full-body deluxe treatment. I'm talking about the works, from head to toe. Mud bath, jacuzzi and sauna, followed by a full body massage and hot oil treatment.

By the time I got to Nina's Nails, I was beyond relaxed. Shit, a girl was floating on top of the clouds. I was finishing up my mani-pedi when my cell phone began to ring the first time.

I didn't even check the caller ID, I just decided to let it go to voicemail. Today was my day and it was going to remain that way. At least, that's what I thought.

I was debating on whether I wanted my hairstylist to touch me up or not, when my phone started ringing again. This time, I thought about answering it, but decided against it a second time.

"Ooooooh! Someone wants to talk to you baaaad," my Asian friend and manicurist teased me.

Before the voicemail actually got a chance to cut on, I checked the caller ID. I didn't recognize the number. So, I followed my first mind and let it go to voicemail. As I was getting ready to put my phone back in my Fendi bag, it started again, from the same number as the two previous times. My curiosity piqued now, so I decided this time to answer it.

"Hello?" I answered.

"Is this Tasha?" the voice on the other line asked. The voice was so feminine, there was no question it belonged to a female.

"Yes, it is. And usually when a girl doesn't answer after the first two times, it means she doesn't want to be bothered by anyone. Especially someone she doesn't know." The phone was silent for so long, I thought whoever it was hung up.

"Hello?" I checked to see.

She finally replied, "Ty'Reese killed Jay, not Bernard."

I must have just heard that wrong. After I got over my initial shock, I asked her. "Excuse me, what did you just say?"

But I didn't get a response. I waited for a second, still no response came.

"I know you heard me loud and clear. Now, if this is some sort of prank, it's not fucking funny!" I snapped.

"This is not a game, nor a joke. The man you knew as Uncle Bernard did not kill Jay. Ty'Reese killed him."

"Wait, wait a minute." I cut her off. "Why would Ty'Reese kill Jay? That doesn't make sense."

"It makes perfect sense. He found out the truth. He learned the truth and couldn't accept it." She told me.

Nina wasn't paying any attention to my nails anymore. She was all caught up in my conversation. I waved my hand hard in her face and she got back to work.

"He learned what truth? Truth about what?" My heart was racing. My breaths came in short bursts.

Could what she was saying be true? Is it possible we killed two innocent people? My mouth instantly became dry.

"I'm sorry, Tasha, I can't talk any longer."

Again, I cut her off. "What do you mean, you can't talk any longer?"

"I'm sorry...I ...must go."

Before I had a chance to respond, she called out, "Meet me at the West Oakland Greyhound Station tonight at ten-thirty pm." Then she hung up in my face.

I was so shocked by the experience, I just sat there with my mouth agape, lost in thought. I hadn't realized Nina had finished my hand, until she began lightly tapping me on the back of my hand to get my attention. I gave her the unfinished hand and picked my cell phone back up and tried to call Jeffrey. I didn't like it when his phone was turned off. However, I knew what the fellas went to Russia for. Because of that, I had to accept that he most likely turned the phone off for security reasons.

I swear, it seemed like Nina did my second hand in five minutes. I know it felt that way because I was lost in thought. She was tapping my other hand, smiling. When she had my attention she told me, "You done."

I gathered my things and headed to the front to pay for my services received. A damn good service. You could tell when you saw my fingers and toes.

The woman's phone call helped me make my mind up not to get my hair retouched up. It was only done a week ago, so I really didn't need it. Plus, after the woman's phone call, I would not be able to sit in no one's chair. Not with what she'd said on my mind. I needed to be somewhere alone thinking about it. I wish Jeffrey would answer his phone.

A few hours later, I found myself driving down San Pablo Boulevard, headed for the Greyhound Station. At 10:30 at night, the Greyhound Station was skid row. Plus, I had no idea who I was meeting. This could be some sort of set-up or something. Because of these facts, I had my 9mm with me, tucked nicely away in my Fendi purse.

I didn't know whether I should park in front on the street, or in the back of the station. I thought about the type of meeting I was expecting and decided to park in the back.

When I pulled around the back, there was one bus out of service and one bus unloading passengers. Passengers moved about, while people of the night roamed around them.

The night was dark and moonless, with hardly a star in the sky. I couldn't help thinking, it would be a perfect night to kill somebody and get away with it. I parked on the opposite side of the two big buses. That way, I was easily seen by anyone who was looking. It didn't take long.

I had just turned my car off and patted the gun through the outside of the purse, when a knock came on my passenger side window. I looked over and saw a middle-aged black woman wearing a wig and a dark jacket. She was hunched over like she was hiding from someone. My instincts told me this was the woman who called me. However, I still scanned the station to see if anyone else was interested in me or my guest. She knocked on the window again. I pressed the unlock button and let her in the car.

"Tasha, you don't have anything to worry about. I promise you; I would not put you in harm's way," she told me as she removed the large pair of Chanel glasses from her face.

She looked familiar. Although I could not place her face, I felt as if I knew this woman.

"And tell me, just who are you?" Knowing who she was, was of the utmost importance.

"Tasha, I'm your Auntie Valerie. Mama J. was my lil sister. She and I have never seen eye to eye about almost everything in life. We were different as little girls and grew completely apart as women. We'd go sometimes five or six years without talking. But we still loved and trusted each other—"

I cut her off. "Okay, but what does all of that have to do with Jay and this person Ty'Reese?"

"Okay, I see. Mama J. told me you were impatient. Okay, let's see. Where do I begin? If you kids did indeed kill Mama

J. like everyone thinks, then I'm sure she told you everything. Well, at least almost everything. My sister always said she felt y'all children deserved to know the truth.

"All of you children are siblings. What happened to those girls was an outright shame that was swept under the rug once the scandal was known. Ty'Reese was her first child born. When he was born, folks sort of looked the other way. However, a few years later, you three little ones were born. At first, the church was in an uproar, then slowly but surely the roar died down. The pastor was put on a sort of probationary period and the roar became a whispered rumor, then forgotten.

"That is, until little Ebony came along. With Mama J. being pregnant again without a man in the picture, the rumor mill kicked right on up. She tried her best to conceal her pregnancy, but with her being the lead vocalist in the choir, that was pretty difficult. As a last-minute gesture to save the church from civil mutiny, Mama J. asked me to keep little Ebony—" Again, I cut her off.

"So, you're telling me, I have a little sister and her name is Ebony? Okay, but that doesn't explain about Jay. And who is Ty'Reese?"

"Ty'Reese is Alex's first name. His full name is Ty'Reese Alexander Watkins and he is Jeffrey's older brother. Somehow, he found out the truth and is hellbent on getting revenge. Ty'Reese killed Jay because of how close he and Jeffrey were. It was his way of getting Jeffrey back for killing Sheila."

"How do you know all this?" I had to know.

"Because Bernard and Mama J. were secretly in love with each other. Bernard would've never hurt Jay. Plus, Reverend Jacobs reached out to me a couple of months ago. He called himself inquiring about little Ebony and how she was doing, but I knew he was full of it."

I weighed what she was telling me over in my head. "How do I know what you told me is true?"

"Because they are trying to kill me, look." She reached inside her bra and pulled out a photo. "Look at my little angel."

She handed me the photo of a little girl who looked to be about nine years old. She was beautiful. The little girl looked just like me when I was her age. She looked so innocent and pure, I just wanted to protect her.

"Please, Tasha, he is going to kill me. I can feel it. But please, don't let him kill my baby. Your organization is pretty strong, I believe...."

BOOM! BOOM!

It took a second to register what happened. Valerie's head exploded from the force of the two bullets that crashed into it. The inside of her head sprayed over everything inside the car.

I pulled my gun from my bag and returned fire at the figure that was about ten feet away from my car passenger side.

BOOM! BOOM!

BOCCA! BOCCA! BOCCA!

We traded shots back and forth.

I had an extra clip for my gun in my bag. Yet, if I remained in the vehicle, I would be a sitting duck. An easy target.

After I fired a barrage of bullets, I quickly started my car. The timing could have not been more perfect. Whoever the guy was that was shooting at me, he was crouching down behind a bus reloading. I used that time to speed out of there.

*** 3X ***

CHAPTER 10

KANE

When Jeff To Da Left called me and told me what had happened to Tasha, he was furious, no he was beyond furious. He was livid. I couldn't blame him either, because if someone would have come at my queen like that, I'd be straight on Michael Myers mode.

Them Neva Die niggaz have a saying. They always say that they got it like Dracula. Symbolizing that they got it in blood. Which is exactly how I would get it if a mothafucka crossed them territory boundary lines.

It was fucked up to hear it was his older brother Alex that had tried to kill Tasha. Hell, I thought Jeff To Da Left's older brother was locked away in jail or prison doing life. Why would he want to bring harm to his brother's woman? That didn't seem right to me. But no matter what, this was Gas Nation on mine and *Revenge Is Promised*.

I gave Jeff To Da Left my word that I would act as bodyguard for Tasha and make sure nothing happened to her. I hung up the phone, grabbed my weapons and was out the door.

It only took me ten minutes to get to their place.

"Who is it?" Tasha called through the door as I knocked. I could hear in her voice that she was scared.

I replied, "It's me, Tash. Sis, it's Kane."

"Kane," I could hear her repeat to herself.

Once she opened the door, I could tell she was trying to mask the fact that she was shaken by looking at her. No matter how hard she tried to mask it, she was visibly shaken. Considering what she had just gone through, I figured now was one of them times when a nigga needed to talk.

"Brah just called me and told me what happened. I came to make sure it doesn't happen again." This seemed to get her to let her guard down.

"Kane, I don't mean any disrespect, but I thought you couldn't talk," she said as I stepped over the threshold.

"Not can't talk, I just choose not to talk on the account of there's a shortage of people out there worthy to talk to. I talk when needed or when I find someone worth talking to. This clearly was one of those times when talking was needed. I would think you needed a friend after what you've been through."

I followed Tasha into the living room. It was the first time I'd ever seen the inside of their place. I had only been on the outside. It was filled with nice furniture, state of the art appliances and electronics. There was African art on the wall and a few plants were spread throughout the living room. The apartment was decked out.

The moment we sat down; I made the mistake of asking her to explain what happened. Her resolve dissolved and she broke down in a fit of tears.

Growing up in the hood, a nigga was used to seeing the ugly face of sorrow. All too often it reared its ugly head on the face of a young mother, wife, sister, or niece of a slain victim. These women being secondary casualties in the game of life that we call "The Streets."

I stood up from the chair I was sitting on and made my way to the couch and sat beside her.

"Sssshh! Don't worry, sis. It's okay now. I got you and I promise you; won't no nigga touch you while I am here." I did my best to calm her down, but my attempts were useless.

I decided to hold her silently until she calmed down or quietly cried herself to sleep. Doing my best to assure her everything would be okay. At least for us, they would be.

*** 3X ***

Jeff To Da Left

Nigga, when the plane landed, I hit the ground running. I wasn't tripping, I was TRIPPING! This mothafucka had the nerve to try and touch my queen. Nothing was off limits, and *Anybody Could Get It!*

The only problem was, I don't know much about my older brother. I hadn't seen him since Sheila was alive. The last I heard he'd received life. Alex always was a mama's boy. Because of that, he and I didn't see eye to eye or get along for the most part.

If he is tripping off that bitch, Sheila, fuck him! That bitch deserved what I did to her and some more. The way she treated me, she was lucky to die the way she did. They always say smoke inhalation kills you, not the fire. But if I could kill her now, I would think of some very creative ways to get the job done.

Anyway, like I said, my problem was I didn't know anything much about my brother Alex. But soon that will change. Last night after tending to Tasha's needs and making sure she was ok, me and the team took to the streets on full beast mode.

It was now mid-morning and me and the team were still lurking. Yeah, I was the schoolboy. They done fucked around and brought out the monster.

"Yo, Left, ain't that two of them niggaz right there?" C1ty called out as two niggaz came walking out of Campbell Village.

"Pull up on them and we gonna pop out and see what's up," I instructed him.

I didn't have to worry about the van following us. I knew they would peep what we were doing and follow suit.

The two niggaz didn't have time to figure out what was what. We swooped up on the curb and I bounced out with a MAC-11 barrel pointed at both of their faces.

C.J. and Lil John, , jumped the curb behind them and bounced as I knew they would, ready to blaze. None of us were worried about the few cars that drove by in the early morning. We were predators who'd have been out hunting all night, only to just now have found our prey.

"What's up wit Blood?" I called out the moment I bounced out the van.

"Man, what the fuck you niggaz want 'round here? You mothafuckas know y'all are in Decepticon Field Play. Nigga, this our territory!" one of the niggaz, a Dru Down lookalike, spit at us.

"My nigga, I promise you, I got one question and you two niggaz can go on about yo business. But as God is my witness, now ain't the time to play gangsta. Try me, nigga, I dare you!" I told them with all sincerity.

The Dru Down looking nigga, looked like I just slapped his mama.

"Nigga, fuck you and that nigga, God. We're Decepticons. We don't answer no fucking—"

TAAAT! TAAAT! TAAAT! TAAAT! TAAAT!

The MAC barrel sang that *rat-tat-tat-tat* song before the stupid son of a bitch could finish what the fuck he was saying.

"Didn't I tell you niggaz I wasn't playing no fucking games?" I asked his dead body.

The second nigga looked like he wanted to shit himself. I knew he'd answer me with no problems, but loudmouth fucked that all up.

"Throw his bitch ass in the van, along with that loudmouth ass nigga and let's go." I ordered.

My goons didn't have a problem carrying out my orders. First, they dragged the live nigga in the van. Once he was secure, niggaz tossed the dead nigga in the van.

A little while later, we were in the basement of one of the trap houses. C1ty was slowly dragging the blade of the machete across a sharpening stone. The nigga, whose name was Red I found out, was tied up in a metal chair crying like a little bitch.

I needed him to know I was not playing games. In case his dead comrade didn't let him know I meant business, slicing his ass up like bacon would. I looked over at C1ty and told him, "Do something to let him know we're serious. Make sure it hurts."

Even though o'boi was already scared, I needed him petrified. He needed to think I was the devil. That way, he would say or do whatever I said.

Red was tied in one of the chairs where you could tie around the chest and tie the forearms down on the arms of the chair. C1ty had a look of hideous pleasure on his face as he walked up to Red.

"Yo! You remember that part of *Shottas,* my nigga, when Mad Max chopped o'boi's hand off and smoked a cigarette with the hand? Now that was some real gangsta shit." Before his words could register in my ears, I saw C1ty swing the machete in a swift arch slicing through meat and bone.

Clank!

The sound vibrated through the air resonating through the basement. A gag forced down Red's mouth muffled his screams. The hand fell to the floor with a thumping sound.

C1ty picked up the limp hand, laughing at a joke only he knew or heard. He took the hand and slapped Red in the face with it. This sent Red over the top with fear. He pissed on himself before passing out. He was ready now.

I walked over to him with a bucket of water in my hands I got out the bathroom and tossed it in his face. The putrid ammonia smell of the urine was very strong. Still when he came to, I stared deep in his eyes for a long time. I could see his broken spirit through his eyes.

I untied the gag from his mouth.

"Do you understand I mean business?" I asked him after I was certain I had his full attention.

He looked like he was on the verge of losing his sanity or on the very brink of insanity itself.

"L-l-look m-man, I'll tell you anything y-you want to hear. J-just don't kill me," he cried as he stuttered, making it almost impossible to understand him.

"Alright. That's good," I told him while pulling up a chair up and sitting directly in front of him. "My first question is a rather easy one for you. Who's the head of the Decepticons?"

Red looked like he wanted to be anywhere but here with me right now.

"Come on, Red, help yourself."

"He'll k-kill me if I t-talk," was his response.

"Red, you remember what happened to your friend? Imagine what I am going to do if you don't talk."

Red bit down on his lip.

"You'll let me go if I tell you?" he desperately asked while sweat ran down his face.

"I promise I won't kill you, Red." With these words, Red gave up everything.

*** 3X ***

CHAPTER 11

JEFF TO DA LEFT

Red confirmed what Ty Dollar-Sign had found out from some toss-up that supposedly tricked off with Phoenix and overheard him one night on the phone. Phoenix was not the head of the Decepticons, he was simply the front man. The true leader of Decepticons was my older brother Ty'Reese. Quiet as it is kept, I didn't need to hear the gossip of some tramp, or confession of a snitch to know the real. Sheila had told me about Ty'Reese when I was in Moscow. I just chose not to listen Apparently; he didn't lose his case. The case I was led to believe he'd received life in prison for, he spent two years in Alameda County's main jail, Santa Rita, fighting the case.

He was in Santa Rita where he learned about Sheila's death, which he took very hard. Apparently, the charges against him were dropped. All Red could tell me was Ty'Reese was out to find out what had happened to Sheila and was ready for revenge if it was foul play.

Shit, all he had to do was ask me. I would tell him I killed that bitch and was happy she was gone. Wasn't any room in the Nation for weakness.

I kept my word to the snitching ass nigga; I didn't kill him. I let him live long enough for C1ty to hack his head off with the machete.

Afterwards, as I was riding back home, it happened again out of the blue. "My son knows what you did, you pussy-ass nigga. And he's going to make you pay." This time, not only could I hear her, but I could see her, in the passenger seat of my Porsche truck.

The shit tripped me the fuck out. But I wasn't about to let that bitch see me sweat.

Suddenly the inside of my truck smelled like burned clothes and burning skin. Her face was ashen where there was skin still on it. The rest of her face was a mixture of pinkish flesh and burnt skin that gave off the appearance of it actually melting. No bullshit, her skin looked like it was melting. I tried rolling the window down some, in an attempt to freshen the air. That shit didn't work.

"Fuck your son, you glass-dick sucking bitch!" I looked at her and told her.

She didn't relent. "You are going to suffer, you festering demon child."

"Festering? Bitch, have you not looked in the mirror lately?" I pulled the passenger visor down and opened the mirror.

Fucked me up. I didn't know a ghost could cry. When she looked at her reflection in the mirror, sure enough, Sheila began crying. It was a gut wrenching, heartbreaking cry. I started to feel bad for her. After all, this was my mother. Had she not given birth to me I would not be alive.

The moment sympathy started to invade my heart a memory invaded my mind. I was only five. Sheila had been on a crack binge for four days and asked me to make her a cup of tea. I was too eager to comply, hoping that would sober her up. I wanted her sober so badly, that I put a ton of sugar in it, thinking that sugar would help sober her up. When she tasted the tea, she spit it out and slapped me and threw the scalding hot tea in my face. That hot liquid felt like acid as it ate through my skin. My neck still held some of the scars from the tissue damage caused by the tea. Instantly my heart froze. The memory reminded me of one of the many reasons I did what I did. All of the horrible things that she did and allowed others to do.

"Naw, don't sit there and cry, bitch. Talk that greazy shit now," I taunted her.

She looked at me like she was going to explode. Finally, she screamed, "I fucking hate you, you fucking faggot!"

Afterwards she was gone. She just vanished the same way she appeared. The god-awful stench left with her, but not completely. Remnants of it still lingered in the truck.

By the time I made it home it was dark, and Tasha was in bed. I jumped in the shower to wash away Sheila's funk, then climbed into bed. I thought my baby was asleep, but when I laid down, she asked, "How was your day, baby?" Her voice was soft and angelic.

I slid behind her and wrapped my arms around her body. "It was a good day, baby. Any day I make it back to you is a good day, regardless of what happened throughout the day."

"Mmm, daddy, you so sweet. Always telling a girl just the right things at just the right time."

"Babe, as I always tell you, I'm just speaking the truth. I can't take credit for that."

She started rubbing her ass against my dick, making slow circles.

"But you can take credit for how I feel, daddy."

"I most definitely can do that," I told her as I thrusted my hips forward, rotating my hips right along with her. When I did this, a soft moan escaped Tasha's lips.

Tasha needed me, and I wanted her. No, I needed her just as badly. She reached her hand in between our bodies and grabbed my erect and throbbing dick. At the same time, my hands roamed her body until they found the slopes of her breasts. Her erect and hardened nipples felt like little rubber bullets to my touch. My breathing got heavy as lust fueled my hunger. I climbed on top of Tasha and took one of her breasts into my mouth.

"Mmm, yes daddy," she moaned as my tongue wrestled with her nipple. My hand made its way down to her hot, wet, waiting inferno. Just when I thought nothing could mess up our mood...

"Look at you! You don't even like girls. I don't know why you are sitting there wasting that girl's time. You're not going to satisfy her, you little faggot, and you know it." Sheila's voice felt like someone pouring a bucket of ice water on my head, instantly killing the groove.

I tried to ignore Sheila and kissed my way down Tasha's abdomen, making my way down to her hidden treasure. When I finally made it, I slid my tongue across the tip of her clitoris.

"Ssss," she moaned as she thrusted her hips upward into my face. I licked her lips from their base to the top and then began sucking on her pearl tongue.

"Mommy, Mommy, don't you leave cause Sissy Boy's got something up his sleeve, and if you leave then I can't sleep, cause Sissy Boy's gonna put his hands on me!" Sheila started singing that shit right in my fucking ear.

I don't know what was weirder, the fact that I could hear and see my dead biological mother whom I killed. Or the fact that she was sitting there, making faces at me while I was trying to do my thing with my fiancée.

"Fuck!" I yelled out in frustration.

"What's the matter, babe?" Tasha asked in a voice full of care.

"You're gonna think I'm crazy."

"No, I won't, daddy. Tell mama's what's wrong."

By now I'd climbed off of her and was sitting down on the bed. Tasha sat up and started rubbing my back. The crazy part is she was starring right at Sheila. Almost as if she could see Sheila herself.

Now that's crazy!

"Babe, I can't get Sheila out of my head. It's like she's right in my ear and she's always talking shit. I am sorry, babe, but a nigga can't do his thing with her in my head." Hopefully, Tasha wouldn't think I was losing my mind.

Tasha took a deep breath like her next words were going to be devastating.

I embraced myself for what I thought was sure to come out her mouth. Instead she shocked me by saying, "Jeffrey, you're not crazy baby and Sheila isn't in your head." She took another deep breath and closed her eyes.

She had my attention now. My full attention!

"Babe, I don't know how to say this, so I am just going to come out and tell you that Sheila's ghost is haunting you, me, us. I don't know, possibly Ty too. But I can see her. I've been seeing her ever since Mama J.'s funeral." Her shoulders slumped after she told me this, like a giant weight was removed from her shoulders.

"Babe, you know I don't believe in all that hocus-pocus, boogedy-boogedy-boo madness. There is no ghost of Sheila trying to spook me. That bitch is just in my head." Yeah, I was talking a bunch of bullshit. I knew it, I just didn't want to admit it.

It was simpler just to say I was going crazy, than to say I was being haunted and spooked by the ghost of my dead mom. I mean, for real, where the fuck they do that at?

Even though I could see Sheila standing by the bathroom door, I acted as if she wasn't there. Well, except I pulled up the cover and covered my dick.

Tasha reached for my hand and took it in hers. "When we were at the funeral, I saw Sheila talking in your ear. Taunting you and challenging you. I didn't say anything because I didn't know how to say something like that. But now I am telling you, you are not alone."

I didn't know if this was a joke or not, but I knew my baby didn't get down like that. Cracking jokes when a nigga was being serious or making fun of a nigga during a delicate moment.

I thought of that *Yatta* song, when he sang about putting his pride to the side and I did just that.

"So, you're telling me that you can see Sheila?" I double-checked.

"Well it started off with me being able to see her. Now I can see and hear her as well."

The look on my face must have spoken volumes of mistrust, because she added quickly, "I heard all the nasty things she said to you."

*** 3X ***

Tasha

Of course, I heard all the nasty shit Sheila said to Jeffrey, but like I told him, I didn't know how to tell him. I could both see and hear Sheila.

"Daddy, I can see that bitch standing by the bathroom door looking all pathetic and shit and I can hear her voice. But for some reason, she doesn't speak to me. Hell, she hasn't acknowledged me at all."

It was my turn to get shocked.

"Tell her, you little faggot, I don't speak to whores! That little shit is the whore of Babylon. I won't stoop down low enough to talk to her. It's no wonder she chose to be with you.

You little faggot." Hateful words just spewed from Sheila's mouth like the stench of bad breath.

"So, you're telling me you heard that too?" Jeffrey tested me.

"From everything you shared with me of her exploits, I say she was the whore, not me." A huge smile came over his face once he heard my words. He was happy to see that I told the truth.

Just then, a bright idea came to me. I leaned forward and wrapped my arm around Jeffrey. "Since she wants to call me names, daddy, let me show her what a good whore I really am."

I stood up from the bed and walked around so I was standing in front of him. Then I placed my hands on his chest and softly pushed him down on the bed. I was focused on finishing what Jeffrey started. I'd be damned if I let a dead bitch stop me from getting me some.

Moving the comforter to the side, I got on my knees and came face-to-face with his magic stick. He was on semi-erect, which meant it was time for me to do my business. I grabbed him by the shaft and slowly began stroking it. While I did this, I let my tongue trace circles around the head of his shaft. Just as I figured, his penis began to grow in my hands. I prepared myself for what I needed to do.

I knew I had my work cut out for me. At full erection, it is about eight and a half inches long. But it is also about eight inches in girth.

"Go 'head, whore, and suck that little faggot's cock," Sheila said trying to taunt me. But one look at his massive, fully erect penis and I was in a trance-like state.

First, I began with the head. Licking and sucking around the bulbous tip and building my courage up to take him in my mouth. Every time I did, it was like a new challenge because of his size.

Finally, I opened as wide as I could and let my mouth almost engulf half of him. My lips were stretched to their max. Saliva flowed from my mouth, around the edges and down his shaft and I began sucking.

My head was rising up and down, making sure I used plenty of spit because I knew that was how Jeffrey liked it.

I put on an extra good show for Sheila, since she wanted to talk that shit!

I was sucking and slurping so loud I couldn't hear anything over my own sounds. It wasn't long before I felt his size grow a little more and his testicles become stiff, letting me know he was getting ready to release. I sped up my pace and sucked a little harder, encouraging him to release in my mouth.

Sheila was calling out all kinds of bullshit, but I was paying her no attention whatsoever. I was making my man cum. When he did it was too powerful for me to swallow all of it. I did my best, but some of the semen spilled out down my chin and down his shaft.

Before Jeffrey could recover, I climbed on top of his still swollen, rock-hard penis. My vagina was on fire from need. I positioned his head at my slippery, wet opening and guided it into me. His girth stretched me to the max. It was torture, yet it was delicious.

Once I'd slid completely down on the top of him, I slowly began to rock my hips back and forth, letting my walls loosen up to receive his full size. He grabbed my hips impatiently, but this was my show. I removed his hands and put my hands on his chest. Then I began to rise up and down on his little monster.

"Ssss... mmmm... daddy," a moan escaped my mouth.

I've never felt myself get so wet down there. I could actually hear the swishing sounds of his cock going in and out of me.

"Oooh, Jeffrey... daddy! Mmm." It was feeling too good. This time when his rough hands found my hips, I didn't bother moving them. Instead, I bit down on my bottom lip and encouraged him.

"Yes! That's it, daddy, fuck me." I moaned in his ear. Jeffrey took hold of me and started fucking me like a porn star and I loved it. When he raised his head and took one of my tits in his mouth, I was lost. "That's it, daddy! Ssss... That's it!" I managed somehow to holler out before I lost complete control in the form of my first orgasm.

Jeffrey didn't let me off that easy. Thirty-five minutes and four orgasms later, he finally reached his orgasm. Neither one of us knows when Sheila had enough of our antics and left. But as I lay in orgasmic bliss, all I know is she was gone.

De'Kari

CHAPTER 12

TY DOLLAR-SIGN

Being in Russia enhanced my need for the finer things in life, and my will to go and get them. On the flight back from Moscow, I made my mind up that I would hit the ground running, like Usain Bolt.

This morning, a nigga did just that. First, I checked on our traps to make sure they were all running smoothly, and the count was correct. After that was done, I met up with a few contacts I'd been sitting on the back burner. A couple turned out to be some bullshit. Yet two was fa'sho lucrative.

Around 1:00 p.m., I decided to grab me a bite to eat, so I headed over to the fish shack to get me some of that good red snapper they got. Most niggaz wanted that catfish, but I'm a red snapper muthafucka.

I pulled into the parking lot slapping that 3x Krazy *Stackin Chips*.

"I'm trying to stack my chips so I can clock a grip/ Then I make some hits and I hate to snitch/ So I sticks to scripts Hit my licks/ It ain't nothing like them big head green dead presidents/

That is the God honest truth. There's nothing in the world like them big-head dead presidents! Nothing like having a pocket full of big faces, just waiting on you to do whatever you want with them. To me that was heaven.

I parked the whip, grabbed my .44 Desert Eagle off the passenger seat and the other off my lap, and tucked them both inside my waist, before getting out of my whip.

With everything that's going on with Ty'Reese, I stay ready, so I don't have to get ready. Fuck around and I'll be the one to transform like Megatron in this bitch!

I guess fate was just itching to test me because I opened the door and came face-to-face with none other than Ty'Reese himself.

"What do we have here? If it isn't little Ty aka Ty Dollar-Sign. I personally like little Ty. It has such a…. What's the word for it? A 'me' sound to it." He broke out laughing at his own joke.

"Nigga, you see a comedian, or a comedy show over here?" I growled, ready to get it popping in broad daylight!

Fuck the customers!

My hands went to my waistline.

"Tsk! tsk! tsk! I wouldn't do that if I were you, little Ty," he said, then made a gesture with his head.

My eyes followed the direction he was leading them. Sure enough four cops were seated at the table no less than ten feet away from us. When my eyes saw them, I dropped my hands back down to my sides.

"Look at you, Ty, always trying to jump the gun. This case literally." This nigga must've really thought shit was sweet. From the looks of it, he didn't even have any security with him.

"We gone catch up to you, fuck boi. And when we do, I'mma show yo bitch ass about jumping the gun." My voice was low and deadly, very intimidating.

Ty'Reese didn't flinch. Says a lot about him. Around the hood it was said that Ty'Reese had a few drills under his belt. Which meant he done put in some work. But he wasn't known as no cold-hearted killer.

I was!

"Uh, do you boys have a problem?" One of the seated cops stood up like he was going to come our way.

Ty'Reese smiled like he was a toothpaste commercial actor. "No, sir! No problem! Me and the lil homie here just catching up, that's it."

I wasn't a fucking actor, so I didn't say shit. I just stared at Ty'Reese.

"Well, little homie, I'mma take you up on your offer sometime later. Trust me, though, I'm fa'sho going to take you up on it!" After those words, he walked past me and outside where it was safe.

I started to follow him. But I knew if I would, the cops would instantly follow me. Fuck around and I'd be in San Quentin or Pelican Bay State Prison somewhere.

Instead, I walked up to the counter and ordered my food. Fifteen minutes later, I was sitting at the same table the pigs were seated at. They'd left out about five minutes ago.

My food was smelling on point as I sat down. I was seated so I could see the dining room as well as seeing the outside parking lot. I scanned both before picking up a bottle of hot sauce and doing my Dougie.

Fifteen or maybe twenty minutes later, I was admiring the look of the drop-top Delta 88 as I was making my way to it. The paint job was so fresh, the car looked wet. Candy Orange Starburst with the coke-white interior, seated on twenty-six-inch Ashantis. The contrast between the wet paint job and chrome rims was sick.

I'd just gotten my baby out of the shop a couple of hours ago. Boy was I turning heads. Almost everybody called out at me, honked horns, whistle or something. It was a good $6,500 spent. Anybody who told you money couldn't buy happiness, never met me.

After starting the car, I found the right song, 3X Krazy's "Immortalized" and pulled out of the parking lot. All thoughts of Ty'Reese were gone and a nigga was feeling like a king with almost half a million dollars of trap money in the truck.

"We on a paper chase I see it through my third eye/ you played it fast so we mobbin push it worldwide/"

Scurrrrrr!

I never saw the van coming up on the passenger side, but when the tires locked up and the door slid open. I knew what time it was. I clutched my Desert Eagle right around the time that they opened fire.

Boom! Boom!

Taata! Taata! Taata! Taata!

Boom! Boom!

I knew I couldn't hang with them. They had TEC-9's or something. All I had was my hand cannons against handheld missiles.

Instantly, I hit the gas and got the fuck on. I flew through the intersection with the van right on my ass.

Taata! Taata! Taata!

I ducked low so none of the bullets would catch me in my dome. Speeding up the street, I could hear the bullets as they bit angry chunks out of the body of my car. Although I was pissed the fuck off about my car, I was still happy they were hitting the car and not me.

Boom! Boom!

"Now what they thought? That I'd give up and get caught / After I- grab the nine and head straight for the vault/ when there ain't never been a battle that I fought and lost/ without my.... opponent being traced out in chalk/ But I still ain't satisfied so peep the rapid fire/ this will be the day I die, fuck rappin, I'll retire/" Keak da Sneak spit as I was in a full-blown, high-speed chase for my life.

The van caught up to me and the TEC's continued to fire, the bullets whizzing and zinging past my head. I knew I was out matched but the hustlah in me had me feeling untouchable. Like I could go up against an army and make it out.

Scurrrrrch!

I swerved and crashed into the side of the van.

Boom! Boom! Boom!

My slugs tore into the chest of one of the shooters. He instantly dropped his TEC-9 and fell backwards.

"I've done adapted to this environment/ Now they can't stop me/ A mob figga Military tactics menace to society/ One of the chosen five/ That lead immortal lives/"

Now it was Fed X, giving me courage and solace. Encouraging me not to give up. So, when the passenger sat on the window sill to shoot. I slammed on my brakes and swerved as hard as I could into the side of the van. As I'd hoped for, he fell out of the van.

Scurrrrrr!

This shit wasn't a game to me! I hit the brakes fast. It was only the driver left in the van. I threw the car in park and jumped out.

"Nigga, you wanna be a gangsta! Huh! Well, here's some gangsta shit for you." Without waiting a response, I emptied the last three bullets into the nigga's head that fell out the window.

When I looked towards the van, it had disappeared!

*** 3X ***

De'Kari

CHAPTER 13

TY'REESE

These little bitch ass niggaz got the game fucked up! I'm more than willing to set the record straight for them. I don't have a problem letting them know this ain't a fucking game, and I'm fa'sho not playing with them.

At first, I was letting them rock with their cocks out. Giving them the false sense of security that they were actually doing something. While I laid back in the cuts laughing at their young ignorant asses.

Although I was sort of treating it like cat and mouse, I was just waiting to turn the heat up. It was easy blackmailing Uncle Bernard and Mama J. to take the blame for Jay's death.

Mama J. seriously believed that I had taken her daughter Ebony. To save her daughter, she was willing to do whatever I told her to do or say. After all, she'd already lost one child.

Killing Jay was payback for her taking in Jeff after this bitch ass nigga killed my mother. The moment I was told what had happened with the fire, I knew it was bullshit. They told me my mother and her boyfriend fell asleep while getting high and partying.

Sheila had never fallen asleep the nights she got high. I don't care if she'd been awake for five days and was on the verge of crashing. The moment she took a booyah, she was wide awake, tweaking all over again. So, it wasn't possible for her to have knocked a candle over while sleeping. But more importantly, Sheila didn't use a candle for a light. She didn't like the smell of burnt wax. No bullshit. Sheila hated the smell of burnt wax. So, what would she need a candle for?

The police knew she was a dope fiend, so they didn't investigate their deaths. They chalked it up to them getting high.

To them, they were just two more smokers who'd ended their life much too soon behind drugs.

As soon as I beat the murder charges I was fighting, I got on my investigative shit. It didn't take me long before things were pointing in Jeff's direction. Soon after I began to suspect Jeff, I heard about his little episode at the funeral. I knew then my little brother killed our mother.

He'd stolen the only person who had truly loved me. So, I took someone he truly loved. We could have left it tied, one apiece. At least we could have, until they killed my pops. One parent I understood, especially because of the way she treated Jeff. I could not understand nor accept my pops dying! For this, we could swap body for body, until all them little mothafuckas were dead.

I watched my shooters as they opened up on Ty Dollar-Sign. I wish I could have seen the look on his face but killahs move in silence. I must be strategic and stay four steps ahead of them and the police.

I stayed long enough to watch my shooters give chase to their prey, I turned off and went on about my business, just like every other citizen was.

It took me thirty minutes to make it back to my place, where I would watch the news about what happened, while eating pizza and watching the Lakers lose to the Celtics.

I haven't even begun to get started.

*** 3X ***

The triple-black Chevy Camaro was nearly invincible. Its occupants were busy smoking a blunt and watching the house across the street. Nothing else on the block gets any of their attention. They are focused on the job at hand.

Three hours after the streets became dark, the two occupants inside the Camaro exited it. Their all-black clothing spoke their business. The Decepticon logo stitched on their right sleeves said whose business they were on.

The two killahs entered the house via the back door, as quiet as death itself. Ironic, because that is what they were there for. To bring death to the house and all its occupants.

They moved in stealth through the house, like two lionesses on the prowl in search for their prey.

There were four bedrooms in all. Two rooms for the kids a guest bedroom and a master bedroom. They'd left a carnage of death in their wake. Two innocent lives were taken, young innocent children. But they didn't care. They'd received their orders and were going to carry them out the fullest.

The one on the right was the leader. His six-three, hundred and ninety-pound build was a complete contrast to his partner's, who was five-six, a hundred and ninety-pounds, and stocky as a full-grown bull.

The two made eye contact and in that moment held a complete conversation. They'd been on missions too many times together. They didn't need to speak. They knew each other's every move and every thought.

The leader opened the door and stepped inside the room. His stocky companion followed. Lil Moe lay in bed with his childhood sweetheart, Janice. Oblivious to the two representatives of death that just entered their sleeping domain.

Lil Moe ran one of the trap houses for Ty Dollar-Sign over on Milton Street. Normally, Lil Moe wouldn't even be home at this time of night. But Janice had been going in on Lil Moe about the amount of time he was spending away from their family. Making Lil Moe decide to have Lil Blood run the spot for three days. As fate would have it, that decision would cost him his life.

As much as the leader wanted to torture Lil Moe, he wanted to get back to his game of *Grand Theft Auto* more. He looked to his accomplice with his pistol in his hand and nodded.

Just that quick, the life left out of Lil Moe and Janice's bodies. No hassle. No foul. No sounds. Even the flash of barrel spray was concealed due to the silencers screwed onto the guns.

The duo left as silently as they came!

*** 3X ***

Jeff To Da Left

"Alright! Fuck it! This nigga must want mothafuckas to turn it up. Then let's go on beast mode! Any Decepticon that we see, it's a green light right then and there no questions asked." I looked around the room, meeting each man's gaze one by one. "It's time to remind these mothafuckas wat this Gas Nation is about. All Gas, No Brakes! Let's get it!"

We were inside a warehouse just outside the industrial part of the city. My man Booker just came through with a new supply of ghost guns. More AR-15's, and AR-15 pistols. He'd also brought something I'd never heard of, called an AR-33. It just looked like candy and I was ready to see what it do. It was fifteen of us in total. We were breaking up into teams of five. Three heavily armed and deadly teams. The plan was simple. We're going to ride around and terrorize any and all Decepticons. When I say terrorize, I mean kill.

"So, we just bagging 'em. We're not going to worry about trying to get no info on Ty'Reese out of them?" C1ty asked as he slapped a 50-stick into one of the AR pistols.

"Fuck info, it's time we sent a message to the entire town! Niggaz need to know our team is not to be fucked with. A nigga been diplomatic for too long. It's time to start fucking some shit up." I could tell they were all with me by the shouts, whooping and hollering that went up.

Burna, Twon, Murda, J-Roc and I all rode in one Excursion, while the rest of the team loaded up in two other Excursions. After loading up, we rolled out. The three team leaders had two-way handheld radios that covered a ten-mile radius, so communication was available if needed. But I wanted complete radio silence unless absolutely necessary.

We rode around in separate vehicles for an hour before finding anyone. The entire time, the niggaz in my ride were talking and telling jokes. I wasn't in a talkative mood. I was tripping. As if what happened to Dollar-Sign and Lil Moe wasn't enough, Lil Moe was a good kid, more like a brother to all of us. These mothafuckas were about to pay for taking the life of one of ours.

Yeah, nigga, I'm tripping!

The moment we saw the car at the red light, we knew whose it was. Megatron actually named himself after the Decepticon leader. Some people had an issue with him naming himself after the Decepticon leader, because he wasn't in command. But Ty'Reese saw nothing wrong with it, therefore no-one could do a thing about it.

His drop-top '72 Cutlass Supreme was famous in the Town. Not only was the Decepticon logo painted on it, but the car's lights had stencils over them, so the lights shined the Decepticon logo.

I could've had Twon pull up on the side of the Cutlass and got my drive-by on, shooting from the passenger seat of the van. But I never did condone drive-bys. Plus, this shit, was personal. Instead, once we pulled up behind Megatron, I bounced out of the stoley with that AR-15 in my hands. Before jumping out, I made sure to tell niggaz to have my back. They were only supposed to bounce out if there was a problem.

If Megatron wasn't so busy rolling a blunt, he would've saw me come or at least been aware of my presence. I just walked up calmly to the car. "What's up wit it Blood?"

The moment he heard me; his foot hit the gas. Megatron knew he had fucked up and was desperate to correct his error. There would be no correction tonight. I raised the AR-15.

Taata! taata! tat! tat! Taata! taata! taata! tat! tat!

The dark night lit up as the flame from the barrel licked the cold dark night.

There was nothing Megatron could do. He was dead before his head slammed down onto the steering wheel. The back of his head and the side of his face were both torn off by one of the 223's. Megatron's foot was smashed down on the gas pedal when he tried to get away. That same foot was stuck down on the pedal. This caused the Cutlass to bolt across the carless intersection, like a missile.

There was no need to follow the car. I already knew the results before the car sped across the street. He couldn't survive a head trauma like that, even if God was riding shotgun in the passenger seat.

I turned towards the Excursion and made my way to the big truck. I arrived back at the truck at the same time the Cutlass jumped the curb and crashed into the window of a store.

Silently, we drove off. The night was just beginning.

*** **3X** ***

CHAPTER 14

JEFF TO DA LEFT

I don't know what the fuck got into Ty'Reese, but I know just what I would be willing to do to show him I wasn't the little kid he remembered. The little kid he used to pick on and beat up all the time

I wouldn't allow myself to lose sight of the big picture. I needed to find my little sister and make sure she was safe and out of harm's way. Out of Ty'Reese's reach.

But tonight, we would continue bringing heat to any and every Decepticon in Oakland and let them niggaz know that this was Gas Nation around this bitch.

We'd just left Fruitvale Station and headed towards the deep East. Decepticons were thickest out in East Oakland so this was our area of focus. The tension in the air was thick inside of the truck as we waited for our next victim.

The night was already lucrative for us though, so far, we hit three drills. Since the sun was coming out, we agreed our fourth drill would be our last for the night. C1ty and C.J. hit me a couple of hours ago, they had to call it a night early, due to M.D. catching four bullets in one of their drills. They were getting him to the neighborhood doctor. Our only consolation was they'd dropped seven Decepticons before our comrade was hit.

After a while we drove down 98th Street and headed to East 14th Street. If we stood a chance to run into anybody, it would be on E. 14th. Sure enough, as we pulled up to the light, we saw two Decepticons sitting in the drive-thru, oblivious to the world and their surroundings.

"How do you want to handle it, brah?" Twon asked.

"I say we bounce out on foot, two go around from the front, the other two hit them niggaz from the back, shutting down any avenue of escape," Murda spoke up.

What the homie said made a lot of sense. We flipped a U-turn on 98th and the four of us jumped out.

Taata! taata! taata!

Taata! taata! taata! tat! tat!

I opened up on the back vehicle, a champagne colored Porsche. I focused my barrage of bullets on the driver's door and window to make sure the niggaz in the truck couldn't drive away and flee the scene. *Naw, niggaz, not tonight,* I thought about them trying to get away in the vehicle.

Taata! taata! taata! tat! tat!

I could hear the niggaz inside the Porsche screaming from the pain of the bullets crashing into their bodies. The screams didn't last too long as Murda stood next to me and sent his own barrage of bullets torpedoing towards the Porsche.

As the bullets flew, we marched towards the bullet riddled SUV hellbent and intent on bringing death to the doorsteps of any and all opposition. It wasn't long before confirmation of death's arrival came in the form of the driver's dead body falling and resting on the steering column and the car's horns.

"Gimme a second while I check and make sure everybody's dead." Murda stepped cautiously but with determination after telling me this.

"Are y'all good?" I heard Lil Blood call out from about twenty feet away.

"Yeah. We're good. Niggaz just verifying the kills," I responded as he and Twon came into view.

One look confirmed it all. Nothing else needed to be said. The entire area smelled like we let off a full display of fireworks. The gunpowder and smoke were beginning to burn my eyes.

The two vehicles looked like something from Desert Storm, due to the amount of bullet holes inside of them.

Fuck a Decepticon, Gas Nation was here!

*** **3X** ***

Ty'Reese

I bet these little mothafuckas were starting to understand just how real this shit was. Everything was nice and sweet when you were the only side up having wins, but shit is a different story when you have to check the scoreboard and find out you are losing or starting to lose. Because believe me I'm just getting started and I plan on winning.

I would've loved to have bagged Valerie and Tasha when they were sitting in the car at the Greyhound Station. But I never suspected the bitch Tasha to up a cannon like a nigga and start shooting at me. Nevertheless, I blew the aunt's head off the next day at her house in Emeryville.

Jeff and his band of misfits have been running around crazy causing mayhem. I let them. Decepticons moved in silence like stealth mode. Which would explain why I'm parked in front of this park, watching Ebony play. I've been here for almost an hour, not drawing any attention to myself. Not to mention, all of my windows were tinted so any nosey Good Samaritans wouldn't notice me.

When I first found out about Ebony, it took me only a minute to track her down. Thanks to Mama J., she was relatively easy to track down. The first place I looked was the obvious, Mama J.'s sisters. I mean, you would think they would have put together a better plan because that was the first place I thought of.

I might have hated Jeffrey for what he did to our mother. But she was different, Ebony was innocent. She wasn't tainted by the ills of life in Oakland and she hasn't been defiled by them yet. I would never hurt her. Never!

When I found Ebony, our resemblance was so close that she didn't doubt it when I told her that I was her older brother. After all the shit went down, I was able to persuade her to come stay with me and she has been with me ever since.

She sank another three-pointer flawlessly, with all net. She'd been doing so for the past hour. Looking like she was in college instead of high school. If she stuck with it, she would make it one day for sure as a basketball star. When you added her good looks with her talent, she was for sure to become a superstar. And she was my little sister.

I must have been daydreaming, cause when I came to, some nigga was on the court talking to her. Even from as far away as I was, I could tell he was a grown ass nigga. With rage boiling in my blood, I grabbed my cannon and jumped out the whip.

All I could think of was, what if this nigga was a threat of some kind? The closer I got, the more I realized my assessment was right, this was a grown ass mothafucka.

My little sister was laughing at something he'd said, but I wasn't laughing. My face read murder, but the nigga couldn't see it, because his back was towards me.

"Serious lil mama, you're so fine, I could make you feel what every grown woman loves feeling like." Did I just hear this bitch ass nigga right?

Instead of responding to him and his lame ass line, Ebony called out to me, "Hey, Brother!"

I swear to God if she wasn't standing there, I would fill his body up with more holes than a cheese grater. I began visibly shaking, I was so pissed off.

He turned around to face me. I may not look much of a threat, but I stared him down anyway. He looked to be in his late twenties or early thirties. Considering that I was barely into my twenties myself, he probably didn't see a threat.

"What's up, big brother?" he asked in an intimidating voice.

It made me smile.

"If you don't get yo bitch ass away from my little sister, I promise you, I'mma blow yo shit back," I told him in a non-threatening voice. He smirked like I was a punk.

The threat for him came when I bowed my head. Only one nigga in the city had a Decepticon logo tattooed on the top of his head and everyone knew exactly who he was.

"Uh-uh... T-Ty'Reese... Ty'Reese, I-I'm sorry, brotha. I didn't k-know this was your sister," he stuttered as he began backpedaling.

I don't know what made me do it. My rage was through the roof. I pulled out my Desert Eagle and aimed for his head. I wanted to pull the trigger so bad. Common sense was telling me not pull the trigger. After all, it was broad daylight. My pride on the other hand, was telling me the nigga deserved it for disrespecting my baby sister and for disrespecting me.

"Ty'Reese, please don't. He said he was sorry." Ebony's voice brought me out of my thoughts.

I looked over at her blinked my eyes twice then looked back towards him.

"Get the fuck out of here fast, nigga. I better not see you over here again!" He didn't need to be told twice.

After he left, Ebony challenged me to a game of one-on-one. Up to eleven points by ones. Of course, I accepted. First, I jogged back to the car to put my cannon up. There was no-way I could play with a cannon that big on my hip. Once I got back from putting the gun in the car, we got down to business.

She was better than I thought, in fact, her level of play impressed me something serious. My baby sister was looking like she was on her way to the WNBA.

Here I was, playing ball like I would play with any nigga, and I was losing the game. I teased her, "You're only winning because I'm letting you."

"I know I know and you're only losing because I'm winning" she shot back. "Now I want you to pay attention while I walk the dog and take the family to church."

She was really laughing at me.

She dribbled the ball under one leg then the other. She hesitated, went one way and dribbled the other, pivoted and went back around me the other way and did a reverse lay-up and scored. All while I was still trying to figure out what happened. Just like that, I'd lost eleven to seven.

I wasn't tripping off of the loss. Hell, by now I was used to it. We'd been coming to the park ever since she shared her love of basketball with me. From day one, I saw her potential and felt it was my job as her big brother to help her reach her fullest potential. After all, she was my little sister.

I helped her gather her stuff and we headed home. Along the way, she questioned me about o'boi.

"Ty'Reese, why did you respond so seriously about that guy talking to me?"

"That nigga was thirty-something years old. There's no way a nigga that age should be talking to you, unless he was your coach or your teacher. And from what I heard as I was walking up, the mothafucka was being all kinds of disrespectful," I answered her, wondering just how far this conversation was going to go. How far was I ready to allow it to go?

"I'm seventeen, Ty'Reese. One day you're going to have to accept it that boys are going to want to talk to me."

"And when they do, they'll be your age. They'll be boys, not some grown ass man. Hell, Ebony, that nigga was older than me!" She was quiet after that for a while. So quiet, I looked over at her to make sure she was okay. Just when I was getting ready to say something, she spoke. "How did he know your name? And why did he get so scared of you after seeing your haircut?" I could hear fear in her voice, and it broke my heart. I never wanted her to be afraid of me. There was no need.

I thought about her question. She was my sister, which meant that she was smart enough to understand. But like I said she was innocent. Pure. I didn't want her corrupted and I damn sure didn't want to be the one to corrupt her.

"Because I've been in the streets ever since my mother started using drugs. The love that she didn't give me I looked for in the streets. Now Ebony, the streets are tough and dangerous, but I survived them and made a name for myself. People respect that name."

"It looked like fear to me," she innocently stated.

"When you get older, you'll learn, sometimes people respect you out of fear. Other times, they fear you out of respect. They are almost one and the same."

She sat with a puzzling look on her young face. No doubt, trying to make sense out of what I said.

I let that sit on her mind and drove on.

*** 3X ***

CHAPTER 15

JEFF TO DA LEFT

I was leaving Santa Rita County Jail after putting some money on Abel's books. After finally being released from the hospital, Oakland P.D. arrested him for being in possession of a loaded firearm. Abel was fuming, but it was just one of them things you had to deal with if you're rushed to the hospital and unconscious. The paramedics that arrived on the scene told the police officers about the gun they found on Abel. Even if they hadn't, the police would have found it, because he was a shooting victim and they were called out. For some reason, they were not giving him a bail. Of course, the moment they did, I was going to have him out of there quicker than a flash. Until his court date next month to address his bail situation, all we could do is wait and keep money on his books, making sure he didn't want for anything.

I decided to swing by Jersey Mike's and pick me up a cheesesteak since I was in Dublin. I was far away from the funk; a nigga was able to drop his guard down. I was only going to relax a little. I really didn't give a fuck where I was. War was war, and I wasn't about to be played or caught slipping.

Since there was room to dine-in at Jersey Mike's, I decided to eat there and really enjoy my sandwich. I ordered the #99 and waited for them to make it. The smells were phenomenal. By the time my food was ready, I was contemplating on ordering another one. That's how good it smelled up in the joint.

It took somewhere around ten to twelve minutes for me to devour the foot-long sub, a bag of Miss Vickie's jalapeno chips and a twenty-ounce Coke. Jersey Mike's is the closest thing to Philly's cheesesteaks that I've come across in California.

On the way out the restaurant, my phone started to ring. Looking at the caller ID. I knew it was my queen calling, "Hello, beautiful," I answered warmly.

"Hey, daddy. I just wanted you to know that I'd gotten back early." She had a doctor's appointment today.

I wanted to go with her, but she assured me that it was a simple "girlie" visit. It didn't have anything to do with the baby.

"That was fast. Is everything alright?" I asked instantly, making sure she was okay.

"Daddy, everything is fine. If something was wrong, they would not have let me leave, let alone leave early," she reassured me.

"How's our little baby doing?"

"Oh, she's fine. She's getting big as a house. She needs to hurry up and come, so I don't have to carry all of this extra weight anymore."

"Did the doctor say how much longer?" I asked as I jumped back on 580 West, headed back to Oakland.

"She said it could be any day, but her guess was the baby would be here next week sometime."

"Then I'll be father to the most beautiful angel on earth." I was beyond excited.

"Hey!"

"Don't worry, my love, you will be the second most beautiful angel on earth." I've always told Tasha that she was the most beautiful angel on earth. But that was about to change. I was one week away from being a father.

"Where you at, daddy? Are you close by?"

"I just left Jersey Mike's. Now, I—"

I know you're bringing me a ninety-nine," Tasha interrupted me. Jersey Mike's was one of her favorite food places. "Baby, you know I got you one without you even asking," I reassured her.

"Thank you, daddy."

"You ain't got to thank me for doing what I'm supposed to do, lil mama."

"I know, daddy." She sounded just as sweet as she did on the first day I met her.

"Babe, I got a move to bust and then I'mma come through."

"Okay, daddy, I love you."

"Not more than I love you." We hung up the phone just as I was exiting the freeway on Dublin Boulevard, the exit before Jersey Mike's. I had to turn my ass around and drive back and grab her cheesesteak. Yeah, I lied. So what? She would get her cheesesteak and love me even more today!

I took her cheesesteak once it was done and wrapped it up inside a sweater I had in the backseat. The sweater would help keep the sandwich warm for a longer period of time.

I also decided to alter my plans. My baby was eating for two. There was no way I was going to have her waiting for her food, while I took care of what I was about to handle. I picked up my phone and called Dollar-Sign.

"What's up with you, brah?" he answered after a couple of rings.

"Shit, I'm on my way back to the area." I let him know I was coming back to West Oakland.

"Fa'sho."

"Check it out though, I need to stop and take Tash something to eat first," I was telling Ty Dollar-Sign as I was pulling up to our spot.

"Take care of sis, I'm already at the spot. I'll be here when you pull up."

"Alright, say less," I told him, then hung up the phone.

Things really have been looking right lately. I hadn't even heard from Sheila in a while. And on the streets, we were one up on the Decepticons. And to top it all off, I am about to be a father. Things couldn't be better.

When I grabbed the sweater and unwrapped the sandwich, it was still warm. Right then a funny feeling overcame me. I reached for my hammer, that I'd just taken from under the seat and placed it on my waist. I looked around, looking for any threats and also for anything that stood out at.

I couldn't find the slightest thing or person out of place. I checked around one more time before deciding that I was tripping and headed up to the apartment.

The apartment smelled of honeysuckle and jasmine when I walked in. Tasha was sitting in the living room singing to herself, while looking at one of the items we had bought for the baby. When she saw me, her face lit up like a Christmas tree.

"Daddy, I thought you had something to do?" she asked me, after giving me one of those kisses that any other day, would end up with us both sweaty and out of breath.

"I do, but that doesn't mean I couldn't take the time and bring my babes something to eat." I held her in my arms feeling like the king of the world. I didn't want the moment to end.

Tasha broke our embrace and asked me, "So, where's my sandwich partna, cause we're hungry."

"Oh, okay! So, now I'm partna, huh?" I joked back with her.

"You gone be a lot more than that, boy, if you don't quit playing with me about my Jersey Mike's Philly cheesesteak."

Laughing, I walked over to the dining room table I'd just passed and picked up the bag I had just sat down. I walked into the kitchen to retrieve a plate and unwrapped her sandwich for her.

"Babe, what do you want to drink?" I called out to her, already knowing what she was going to say.

"Sprite!" she responded, just like I'd figured.

Moments later, I came walking out of the kitchen with her food and drink in my hands. Tasha was already seated at the dining room table when I came back.

"Jeff, you're such a good man, and you're going to be an excellent husband and daddy." She smiled at me.

"What you mean going to be? I am already excellent." I added as I bent down and kissed her stomach.

I didn't want to keep Dollar-Sign waiting too long. I kissed my Tasha one more time and told her I would be back as soon as I finished with Ty.

"Tell my brother I said hi," was all she said. Then I left.

Twenty minutes later, I pulled up in front of the trap. Our little niggaz keep the trap jumping all day. It was mid-day, yet the smokers were out like it was the middle of the nightlife. Three little niggaz were serving them, while two other niggaz were on point, looking out. No doubt both of them were holding something big enough to knock down *Andre the Giant*.

"What's up, Big Homie?" Twon, one of the shooters called out to me as I made my way across the yard.

"You know me, Lil Homie, I got money on my mind and money in my eyes," I responded as I climbed up the porch.

Again, that feeling that came over me at my spot just a little while ago, came back. I stopped midway up the porch, turned around and scanned the area.

"Something wrong, Big Homie?" Twon asked instantly, ready to go.

I scanned every car, every person, and everything around. "Naaw, it's all good, Lil Homie. I'm just being cautious and making sure I stay on point," I told him once I saw nothing was wrong.

But something was wrong, I just didn't know what. Call it a sense of doom or whatever, but something was wrong. I shook the feeling and pressed into the trap, I had business to handle.

"Jeff To Da Mothafuck'n Left!" Ty Dollar called out as I entered the room.

"Dollar-Sign, what's good?" I greeted my brother from another mother literally.

He was seated at the table with Lil Blood, C1ty, Twon and C.J. I greeted everybody at the table before taking my seat.

"Where Kane at?" I asked as I sat down.

"Nigga ate off that roach coach taco truck off of West Grand. Nigga done been on the toilet ever since," Lil Blood told me while everybody started cracking up.

"Didn't that nigga learn his lesson from last time fucking wit that truck?" I joined in on the laughter.

Not even two months ago, he'd bought a Super Burrito from that same truck. The nigga fucked around and stayed in the bathroom for two days, shitting and throwing up. I guess he didn't learn his lesson.

Anyway, we had business to discuss and we couldn't sit around waiting on Kane, when we already knew how that could turn out.

It was Dollar-Sign's show and he spoke up.

"We all know this mothafucka Ty'Reese has become a major mothafuck'n problem. Him and them faggot-ass Decepticons. Wasting our time and resources going to war wit his bitch ass is costing us too much." He paused for a minute, looking at everybody seated at the table.

"Tonight, we 'bout to bring this motherfuck'n shit to an end. For a month or so now, I done had a little bitch slide up under him. At first, I was doubtful of her being successful given the time it was taking. Turns out I was wrong. The little bitch managed to get in super close. She's been at the nigga'z house twice already and is going for a third time tonight." Every nigga at the table was looking at Dollar-Sign like he had three heads. Including me.

"The little bitch already shot me the address, it's over in Skyline Hills. She's gonna dope him up to make shit that much easier. After tonight, that mothafucka ain't gone be a fucking problem and then we can get back to the money."

"How sure are you that you can trust the broad? I mean how you know she ain't flip and is setting us up?" It was Kane who'd just come down the hall that asked the question.

"Cause the bitch is Valerie." That put an end to that debate.

Valerie was Dollar-Sign's main thing. Although he had a bunch of women, he and Valerie had been fucking around since for about as long as Tasha and me.

"Now that this is settled, let's get down to how we gone fucking murder this faggot," C1ty spoke up.

Ty'Reese was my big brother and all, but I couldn't agree with C1ty any more than I did on that statement. We spent the next hour and a half discussing what was the best way to deal with Ty'Reese and get this shit over.

At that moment, I'd made my mind up. I was going to turn the reigns over to Dollar-Sign. I'm done. I only got into the streets to find and kill Jay's murderer. Tonight, we would do that. There was no better time with the baby coming. Plus, I had a little over a million put up. Which was more than enough to give me, Tasha and the baby a nice start.

I'd tell Tasha tonight once I got home. I know she will be happy as fuck. I'mma wait until after I tell Tasha to tell Dollar-Sign. Ever since we were kids, he's wanted to be top dog. So, I know he's going to love my decision.

CHAPTER 16

JEFF TO DA LEFT

It was a little after 10 pm when we pulled up in front of the complex. We'd decided that Kane would sit this one out. For one, we had more than enough manpower and secondly, we didn't need to be worrying about being in the middle of this drill, and him all of a sudden needing to take a shit.

C1ty and C.J. were docked out on the block. They'd left right after the meeting and drove out here anyway just to make sure Valerie didn't flip.

This shit is real and niggaz play dirty in the war!

That left Twon, Lil Blood, Dollar-Sign and me rolling. C1ty and C.J. would stay incognito, watching the perimeter in case niggaz rolled up once we were already inside, trying to get us on some "box-in" shit.

We waited until Dollar-Sign received his text message from Valerie that everything was all clear. We all checked our weapons. When we finished, we climbed out of the black Lincoln Navigator. Out of habit, the three of us scanned the neighborhood.

There was no need to hide. Valerie told Dollar-Sign that Ty'Reese never brought any security home. Also, the arrangement they had was she would send a text after the drug had already began to do its job.

We walked up to the front door. Again, for I don't know how many times, that fucking feeling hit me. But it hit me super hard this time. Something was wrong.

"What's up, Big Brah?" Dollar-Sign whispered. All of our guns were out cocked and loaded.

"Something's wrong," was all I said.

"What you mean? The doorknob is unlocked. We're good to go."

"I don't know, but it's a feeling... I've been having it all day. But I'm sure something's wrong with this play."

Dollar-Sign and Lil Blood exchanged looks before Blood asked me, "What you wanna do?"

"Shit, we done come this far. Just be on your toes." It was all I could say because I wasn't turning around and fucking this opportunity up.

"You sure?" Dollar-Sign asked.

I turned and looked behind us. That wasn't it, whatever it was that was causing the feeling was inside the apartment.

"Yeah, let's go." To confirm I was sure, I twisted the doorknob.

I slowly pushed the door open. The inside of the apartment was pitch black. Lil Blood was the first one through the door followed by Twon, Dollar-Sign and then me. Without a word, we moved like a trained military unit.

We noticed someone was on the front couch. This was weird, because the front room was pitch black, and who the fuck would be sitting in the pitch-black dark? Lil Blood signaled for everyone to stop while he checked it out. But all I could think was, it didn't make sense. Where was the bitch?

It was too quiet. Not that quiet is weird, but that the house was dead silent.

We watched as Lil Blood crept up behind the person on the couch. From the position the head was in, they could be sleeping. Lil Blood slowly moved into position. That's when it hit me. The coppery metallic smell of blood. Something or someone in here had been bleeding.

Just as that revelation hit me, Lil Blood signaled the person on the couch was a corpse. We all got closer to the couch.

The closer we got, the stronger the smell got. Dollar-Sign walked over in front of the couch to investigate.

All of a sudden, a gut-wrenching sound escaped Dollar-Sign's mouth. Fuck this shit. I found the light switch and turned it on. Valene was sitting on the couch with her throat slashed.

I moved closer to Dollar-Sign. I told Lil Blood and Twon to check the rest of the apartment, although I knew Ty'Reese wasn't here.

"Val, I'm so sorry, babe. I should've never put you at risk. Me and my stupid self, a nigga was being selfish...."

As I stood there, my brother was down on his knees, crying while talking to Valerie's dead body. Standing there, I felt like he needed his space. However, I needed to know my brother was okay. My heart swelled for his loss.

Hearing footsteps coming from down the hall, I turned around. Lil Blood and Twon were coming back. From the way they were walking, something else was wrong.

"What's wrong?" I asked them. No one responded.

The looks on their faces were like they had seen a ghost back there or something. Still neither one of them spoke.

"Lil Blood, come on, my nigga. We gangstas, it can't be that bad, Cuzzo. What's back there?" Anger was beginning to replace curiosity.

Lil Blood looked at me and opened his mouth, but nothing came out of it. When he tried again, but couldn't, he just dropped his head and started shaking it.

I couldn't take it any longer. With that "fuck it" mentality of mine, I stormed down the hallway, Desert Eagle in my hand, ready. There were only two rooms. The first was empty. I made my way to the second room. The door was already open. Immediately, the smell of blood hit me like a brick wall. It was a lot stronger, which tells me more blood was shed.

De'Kari

There was a queen size bed in the middle of the room. Right away, I could see the body that was laying on the bed. Something was familiar about it, but from that distance I couldn't tell what. Then that feeling came back. This time it was choking me. That's how strong it was. I could feel doom weighing down on me, crushing my shoulders.

I thought of the hesitance in Lil Blood and Twon to speak after seeing whatever was on that bed. Suddenly, I became apprehensive. My breathing became heavy. My body took a step forward, while my mind was telling me to turn around.

One step became another followed by another, which got me close enough to view the hideous carnage. My heart sank in my chest. Dreams shattered as my soul screamed out!

I didn't have the resolve that Dollar-Sign did. Forgetting where I was and why we were there, I let out a mighty roar of a cry.

Why? How? It couldn't be. Sprawled out in front of me was the love of my dreams. Tasha lay lifeless on the bed with our unborn baby in her arms. Tasha's face was barely recognizable, it was so swollen from being beaten severely. She was a grotesque image. A far cry from her normal beautiful self.

After the beating, whoever did this crushed the side of her skull in. The baby was cut from her body, with the womb still wide-open. Baby Evon's head was bashed in as well.

My eyes flooded with a torrent of tears. This had to be a cruel joke. Some kind of sick twisted joke. My family could not be here before my eyes, laid out, tortured in death. All I could do was rush to my baby's side.

*** 3X ***

Ty Dollar-Sign

It was the mothafuck'n sirens that brought out of my stupor. I couldn't fucking believe the bitch ass nigga Ty'Reese killed Valerie. I was seeing angels and demons and all kind of shit as far as revenge goes. Already, I could taste this bitch ass nigga'z blood on my tongue.

Twon had been trying to shake me out of my stupor. Now that I was out of it, I asked him, "Where's Jeff and Blood?"

He shook his head hanging it low. "Man, Ty, it's ugly as hell. Tasha's back there and they cut the baby out of her."

I didn't have time to think. I rushed to the back to my big brother and big sister. I know Jeff was wounded, but we had to go. He was actually in the bed with his family speaking incoherently when I made it to the room. Lil Blood was calling him, but he wouldn't dare step foot in the room.

The sirens were getting closer. If I didn't get him fast, we were all going to prison for a long ass fucking time. I walked up to my brother.

"Jeff, we got to go, Blood. I know you hear them sirens. If we don't leave now, we're going down for this," I told him.

I don't care about going to jail! That bitch ass nigga took my family, my reason for living," he responded back.

"So, let's go make his bitch ass regret ever doing that! If we get locked up and he gets away, that'll be some bitch ass shit!" Now this got his attention.

Though he looked at me like he was death himself, he kissed Tasha on what I guess was her cheek, said he loved her, and we got up out of there. Just in time too. To Da Left's clothes had so much blood on them, that had the police seen us, they would have put us up under the jail.

The ride back to the trap was quiet. We were almost there when To Da Left told us to take him home. He said he just needed some time to himself. Shit, a nigga could understand that

We changed courses and dropped him off. Next, we headed to the trap. I know a nigga should've gone home but being around Tiesha wouldn't have felt right. Not after tonight. Tonight, I had Valerie on my mind.

*** 3X ***

CHAPTER 17

TY'REESE

That shit was fucking hilarious. With the cameras I installed throughout the unit, I was able to watch the entire scene unfold in real time. Them little fuck niggaz thought this shit was a game. Now they're running home with their tails tucked between their legs, with tears and snot running down their faces.

I can't believe they thought a "G" like me would fall for the oldest trick in the book. I'd met the little bitch at this little strip club over in Frisco. Off the top, my sensors were up. Shorty was throwing it just a little too hard at the kid. I knew it was a cross. I just played my position and waited to see how things would unfold.

The first night she came over to my spot on Skyline, I got me some A-1 pussy. Afterwards, she went to the bathroom to clean herself up, and that's when I bugged her phone and purse. I was even able to download one of them cloning programs and cloned her phone. After that, everything else was a simple walk in the park.

The problem with niggaz who think they want to play the game on a serious level and still stay in the hood, they forget niggaz will always know where you live, or could easily find out. I've been knowing were Jeff and Tasha stayed since they first moved in. I could've reached out and touched Jeff whenever I saw fit. I never did because he needed to learn a lesson after what he'd done to my mother. So, I decided to kill him slowly and hit him where it hurts.

I lay on my bed, smoking a blunt of that Gorilla Glue and watching the video I had of them discovering their bitches' bodies. Two niggaz became bitches over their bitches. I just thought that was fucking hilarious, no, fuck'n comical.

Now I was eager to see what they wanted to do about it. Nigga, fuck Kevin Gates. I was ready to die 'bout it! I know if a nigga killed my bitch, I'd be ready to lift heaven and hell to avenge my bitch.

Speaking of my bitch, here she comes now. She's a bad little, Japanese and black bitch, with a hint of Spanish. Five-three, a hundred and twenty-five pounds. I'll say it again, she is one bad mothafucka. She made her way out of the shower over to the bed, still dripping wet. I didn't mind as she climbed on top of my silk sheets. The first thing she did was grab my dick and put that mothafucka in her mouth. I put the blunt to my lips and inhaled. Next, I thought about how sweet it was that they were crying over their bitches and I was getting some head. That was some funny shit.

*** 3X ***

Jeff To Da Left

I can't believe this shit. No, I don't want to believe it! How could my baby be gone? How did I let this pussy ass nigga take her away from me?

It was my fault. I knew this and it's what made everything that much harder to accept. Talk about a big pill to swallow.

Even now though I know God is real. I mean look at it. All day, he was trying to put me up on game as far as what this bitch ass nigga was up to. I just wasn't reading the signs. My head couldn't wrap around the feelings I was experiencing.

The police were the first to call. I wasn't in the position to talk when they did. Even if I was, I would not have talked to them. I know them bitches be trying to misinterpret everything a nigga says. The hospital called not too long ago. It still felt dreamlike.

To make matters worse, Sheila's bitch ass has come back. She's been in my fucking ear taunting me ever since I walked into the door. I swear to God, I feel like I'm going crazy. I need to get up and get out of these bloodied clothes. The hospital needed someone to identify the body and Ms. Carla told them she wasn't up to it.

Poor Ms. Carla. I made a mental note to stop by and go see her. Ms. Carla was good peoples. I don't know what I'm going to say to her. I told Ms. Carla I would protect Tasha from the streets, now look.

I finally got up and hopped in the shower. I made a mental note to deal with the clothes when I got back from the hospital. Part of me wanted to keep her blood on me. It was like a part of her was still with me. Washing the blood off me was like washing her off of me.

The trip to the hospital was made in a daze-like cloud of pain. No matter how many times I told myself that I was going to have to man-up so I could kill this pussy ass nigga Ty'Reese. My heart made me want to man-down!

I hated hospitals with an extreme passion. The last time I'd been to a hospital was when my nigga Linell burnt both his fucking legs. Crazy ass nigga was Bar-B-Q'ing with gasoline. Somehow a fire ember found its way on the tip of the gasoline can. Needless to say, the fire spurted out of the tip like a Roman candle.

Instead of tipping the can over and allowing the gasoline to pour out, this nigga kicked the fucking can like a football. The force of the blow shot the fire infused gasoline all up and down that nigga'z legs and his left arm. Don't get me wrong, looking back on it now the shit was funny as fuck. But back then it wasn't a laughing matter, my nigga had to have like four surgeries.

I made the long trip down death's corridor, until I found myself outside of the double doors that read *Coroner*. Now was the moment of truth. The office next to the Coroner's is where I found the doctor. He was a little, grizzly, grotesque looking man, a little shorter than me. His handshake was cold and clammy. Looking into his eyes, they were cold and dark, like staring into the eyes of a snake. He even slithered like a snake when he moved, slow and silently.

I followed him as he made his way to the morgue. In front of the double doors, I stilled myself and prepared for what I was about to encounter. I knew I could never get myself ready for what I had to do. So, I prepared myself the best I could.

The room was cold and lonely. My baby laid on the table covered in a sheet. She was naked, laid out on a fuck'n cold, steel slab.

"Mr. Watkins, you can take as much time as you need. Just let me know when you're ready," the doctor said.

"Yeah, I'm ready," I responded to his question.

In response, the doctor reached for the sheet that was covering Tasha and began to pull it backwards, until her entire head, neck and shoulders were exposed.

Reality sank in like a wrecking ball crashing into my chest. I couldn't stop the tears if I wanted to. The tears took over me. I cried for so many reasons. We were supposed to do so many things. Now it was all gone. Stolen by a bitch ass nigga.

That soft shit ended right then and there. My tears dried up! A grieving husband was just put to rest. A raging, wronged beast was just let out of the cage. It was time to murda some shit! Time for me to wake Ty'Reese's game up.

I turned around and ran right into Oakland P.D. It was two plain clothed detectives looking like they wanted to get all up in my shit.

"Mr. Watkins, if you have a moment, sir, we would like to have a word with you about Miss Robinson and her tragic, horrendous and untimely death?" the shorter of the two asked. I neglected to mention the shorter one was a woman. You would've figured she would be more understanding, considering she was a woman.

"I don't have no time for y'all. I don't know what happened to my baby. But I promise you, I'm gonna find out and take care of whoever is responsible for what happened to my queen!"

"Are you sure you don't already know? I know you're looking for revenge. You and your *Gas Nation* crew. Mr. Watkins, don't think we're stupid. We know what you guys have been up to. You're leaving a string of bodies across this city a mile long. Stay out of this and just let us take care of everything," her partner spoke up, having the nerves to try and sound like he gave a fuck.

"If you got something on me, partna, I advise you to book me. If not, then you need to get the fuck out my way." I didn't wait for him to say shit. I brushed past him and left out of the morgue, giving the doctor my confirmation on the way out.

I couldn't help but think that detective was abso-fucking-lutely correct. I was about to set the city ablaze. The past year or so, our numbers have grown immensely and I'm about to release the entire Gas Nation onto the city, until we find that bitch ass nigga.

I walked out of the hospital feeling like the devil himself. I picked up my phone and punched in Dollar-Sign's cell phone number.

Dollar-Sign answered with a slurred speech. "Whass up, Biggg Brah?"

Ty Dollar-Sign was taking things hard as well. The four of us grew up as friends, but our bonds became as tight as they possibly could. Only to find out that we were brothers and sisters. And then to start losing one another.

"Brah, how you holding up?" I asked him.

"Not gone lie to youss, I'm fucked up." He sounded like he was on his second bottle of Henn, but he'd be able to sober up and get active.

"Call the fellas. We're going out tonight." I unlocked my Navigator and climbed inside of it.

"Now that's what the fucks I'm talking about! Who you want me to call?" I could hear the news sobering him up a little. His voice was angry and hungry.

"Call everybody we got. I'm done playing Black Ops with this nigga. We in the field and we moving mean!"

"Alright, say less. I'm on it," Dollar-Sign replied.

"Good, let's all meet in the Jets. I want mothafuckas to know what time it is. Nigga, God forgives, we don't!" I ended the call turnt the fuck up and ready to go.

I was so juiced. I didn't even look where I tossed my iPhone. I just tossed it!

"Fuck yo forgiveness! Bitch ass nigga!" When I heard those words, I knew exactly who was speaking. I had got caught slipping. As I lifted my eyes to the rearview mirror, the cold steel of the barrel pressed against my head.

"Nigga, did you think you could kill my mother and I wouldn't do shit?" My brother Ty'Reese whispered in my ear. "Nigga, fuck you and that bitch too!"

Boom!

The pain I felt was immense. It felt like I was just rocked upside the head with a sledgehammer. The loud ringing in my ears wouldn't stop. Did this pussy ass nigga just shoot me? I tried to move, but I couldn't.

"Nigga, now you can say hello to yo bitch!"

BOOM! BOOM! BOOM!

Everything went black!

*** **3X** ***

De'Kari

CHAPTER 18

TY DOLLAR-SIGN

"Man, I know brah-brah ain't got us out here on no 'Ghost Recon' shit," Twon said as he rolled his second blunt

"Come on, nigga, brah ain't neva been on that kind of hype, so don't be getting at him like to that. Shit, nigga look what the fuck he just went through! Lost his whole fucking family tonight and yo ass sitting up in this bitch complaining and talking shit! Nigga, where they do that at?" I was pissed the fuck off, tired, hurt and some more shit!

I wasn't in the mood to be listening to nobody talking shit. Especially about my brother, "Now you niggaz just make sure that you're on point and ready when he gets here. Cause fa'sho brah coming.

I picked up my phone and called To Da Left one more time. It wasn't like him to call us together and not show. When he told me earlier to get everybody together, I did just that. Now we all have been waiting here for three hours without hearing a peep from him.

"Hello?" Whoever it was that said hello, it for damn sure wasn't my brother.

"I don't know who the fuck this is, but you need to put To Da Left on the phone, partna!" I said as harsh as I could.

"This is Detective Lontice Stewart of the Oakland P.D. Homicide Division—"

I quickly interrupted him. "Fuck outta here, copper! What the fuck is you answering my brother's phone for?"

"I'm sorry, who am I speaking with?"

I was beginning to lose my temper. "Didn't I just tell you I'm his brother?"

I'm sorry, sir, but in order to release sensitive information ,I need a name." Detective Lontice didn't give a fuck about sensitive information. He was just being a prick. We all know who he is and how he gets down.

My name is Tyrone McNight, I am Jeffrey's little brother. Now I would kindly appreciate it if you tell me why you are answering my brother's phone." My first thought was To Da Left caught up to Ty'Reese and killed him but got caught slipping.

His next words erased those thoughts entirely.

Mr. McNight, I regret having to inform you that Mr. Watkins is dead. He was murdered outside of Oakland's General Hospital earlier this evening..." He kept on talking but my ears, my body and my soul were fucking numb. I didn't hear anything else.

Murda was the first to notice the change in me. "What's up wit it, Blood?"

I just shook my head slowly for a long time. How did this fuck nigga do it? The devil must've been playing cruel jokes on a nigga. How did we go from *Three the Hard Way* plus Tasha, down to just me?

Naaw, this had to be a mistake. He said it was at General, I needed to see this. I wasn't the gangsta out of the clique, but if a nigga was playing one type of sick joke, I was about to get off into some gangsta shit! Fa'real, fa'real!

I broke out of my stupor. I needed to see it in order to believe it. Jeff To the Left was more than just my best friend or brother. He was my mentor. I've always wanted to be just like him.

Without a word, I grabbed my cell phone and my Mack II and bolted out the front door. I was followed by eighty-four of Oakland's worst degenerates. We were beyond ready to murder some shit.

"Dollar-Sign, what's the business?" C1ty caught up to me as I reached my all-black Chevy Nova.

"Blood, I don't know. I just called To Da Left and Homicide answered his phone, talking about how he was killed a few hours ago. I'm pushing by General Hospital right now to see if it's true." The words sounded foreign as they came out of my mouth.

No matter how much I didn't want to believe it. The shit was making sense. The last time I talked to To Da Left was a few hours ago. Me knowing him the way I did, I know if he assembled us to be at the spot, then he would've been here unless he couldn't be.

After the death of Tasha and the baby, the only thing that would've stopped him from revenge was God and death! I know this for a fact.

"Fuck Blood! Naaw!" was all my little cousin could say.

We hopped in the Nova and burnt rubber headed towards Oakland General.

We were almost there when my phone started ringing. I didn't even check the caller ID. I just picked that shit up.

"Who this?"

Dollar-Sign, my nigga, it's me... Scarface," he answered.

Scarface was our Norteño homeboy, from MMN, Midtown Menlo Norteños, over across the bridge. Him and his team of killahs would link up with us from time to time to get some shit done. I'm talking about everything from selling dope to putting in some work. If it was about that money, them niggaz were B.T.A., *Bout That Action*. All day, every day.

"Face, now really ain't a good time, my nigga." I really wasn't trying to say too much.

"Naaw, my nigga, say less. The streets are already talking, my nigga. I'm just tryna see if you need our help, because my niggaz and I stay ready. On the strength of To Da Left, my nigga, we will do this shit for free, my nigga." I'd never heard him sound so animated yet sincere.

Hearing that the streets had begun talking was like confirmation itself. Don't get me wrong, the ghetto grapevine has been a time or two before. But nothing of this magnitude. Usually when the grapevine get shit wrong it was some "nobody gives a fuck" shit.

"Good looking out, my nigga, that's all the love. Right now, I'm pulling up to the hospital to check shit out. I'll hit you when I know something." I told him as I was pulling into the hospital parking lot.

Our bond with the MMN was because of Jeff To Da Left. So, I know Face wasn't on no fuck shit. The bond began when Jeff To Da Left met a nigga named Fat Boi. They met during a stint in Juvenile Hall and the bond has been Super Glue tight ever since. Although their hood was MMN, they brought the majority of the Norteño nation with them if they aided us.

"Alright, my nigga, keep that shit G and I'mma be waiting on yo phone call."

"Aaight, one." I hung up the phone.

Just then I noticed yellow caution tape at one end of the parking lot. My foot slowly began to ease off the gas pedal. I glanced over at my little cousin and could tell that he didn't want to find out either. It's like the both of us wanting something or someone to turn back the hands of time. Because the caution tape was screaming out to us that it was true.

I pushed on down the parking lot. A long string of vehicles followed me. Then, as if I needed a full-on slap in the face, I saw my brother's Lincoln Navigator with more yellow tape surrounding it.

I knew I couldn't show weakness at all. I had an army of young killahs behind me and they were going to all look to me for leadership.

I pulled up and parked.

"Fuck, Blood," was all C1ty could say.

"C1ty, check me out, cousin. When we step out of this mothafucka, all these niggaz gonna be looking towards you, Kane and me, for guidance and leadership. Even Murda and Twon. Them niggaz is killahs but they ain't leaders. So, you gotta have your game face on. No weakness! No remorse! No bitch shit! We gotta lead this mob, cousin." I was determined to make Jeff To Da Left proud. I would avenge my brother.

"I got you, cousin. Don't trip, Blood," he responded by picking his all-black 9mm up and cocking one in the chamber.

I picked my Glock .40 up from under my seat and did the same thing. Next, I tucked it in my waistband and stepped out of the Nova.

The first thing I saw was the blood and brain matter that was sprayed all over the windshield. As I stepped closer to the truck, I saw more blood inside all over the front seat. I could hear the mumblings of the team as they no doubt put two and two together.

Standing there glaring at where my big brother was just killed, all I felt was the heavy weight of my Glock .40. All I could think of was revenge!

I turned around and made my way through the night into the hospital. We'd come in through the doors that led to the emergency room.

"Uh, excuse me. I'm trying to talk to someone about my brother, whom I believe was murdered just outside a few hours ago," I told the big, black receptionist. She looked like the girl that played in *Precious* and the TV show *Empire*.

"I don't care...." she started to say, until she looked up and saw the look on my face and the number of killahs behind me.

"Uh, I'm sorry this is the E.R., what you need is the morgue. Hold on for one second, I'll call Dr. White and he can assist you."

"Thank you." I turned around and found a spot up against the wall to wait.

I never understood why people who worked in public service were always so rude and mean, like it was everybody else's fault that they chose to be a civil servant.

The entire E.R. was silent as they looked around at the Gas Nation. Eighty-four stone-hearted killahs standing in any room would make anybody scared or nervous. Especially to the average "Joe-Blow" civilian who wasn't in the street life. But was close enough to it, to know what the street life would do to you, if you crossed it.

Ten minutes later, I was beginning to start wondering if maybe Dr. White was coming from another hospital or something. Just as I was going to move from the wall, I noticed Detective Lontice walking my way.

"I'm guessing by the way you move and leading this army, that you just happen to be little brother Tyrone." He came walking up with a smug look on his face and a smirk.

"Look, cop, I'mma tell you one time only. I'm not in the mood for your bullshit and I ain't got time for no bullshit. What do you want?" I really wasn't in the mood.

"Okay, Ty Dollar-Sign. You wanna be a little shit. I'll be a shit. It looks like your little Gas Nation is losing the fight against the Decepticons. Let's say we join forces and bring Ty'Reese down."

"Man, if you don't suck my fucking dick! How you sound, me working with the police. You got a better chance getting Donald Trump to embrace immigration."

"Oh, so you're a smart ass! Would you be such a smart ass if I search you and find that trusty little Glock .40 that you love to carry?" He should've never challenged me like that in front of my niggaz.

I stepped off from the wall, getting directly into his face. "What makes you think that me or any of my niggaz is gonna let you search any of us to find out?" I was so close to his face I could smell the coffee on his breath.

Seeing that we weren't about to back down nor buckle, Detective Lontice didn't know what to do. He was saved by Dr. White.

"Excuse the display of testosterone, gentlemen, but I'm looking for the family of the deceased," Dr. White spoke up.

Reluctantly I broke my stare from Detective Lontice and looked at Dr. White. "Hello, Doc, that's me." I extended my hand.

"I'm terribly sorry for your losses." He took my hand and shook it. I knew he was talking about Tasha and the baby, as well as Jeff.

"Yeah, Doc. It's been one hell of a day."

"Well, if you're ready, we can go back to the morgue and tend to the unfortunate business at hand."

I looked over to Murda and Twon and then back to Detective Lontice. Both of my goons gave me a head nod. Message received loud and clear. If Detective Lontice so much as farted, they would gladly air his punk ass the fuck out with no hesitation. Our niggaz lived for that gunplay. I mean, with a name like Murda, what the fuck would you expect?

I turned around and gave C1ty the next look and a head nod, this let him know he was in charge. Then I followed the good doctor.

*** **3X** ***

CHAPTER 19

TY'REESE

I'd just killed my little brother Jeff. I'm supposed to be off somewhere wallowing in sorrow or some shit. Not me, play-boy, I move to the sound of a different beat. That humdrum, when it gets to beating won't allow me to let up as I go full throttle. These little niggaz started this war and I'mma bout to make sure that I end it!

See, a lot of niggaz got this shit fucked all the way up, talking about they not killing no women or children. Nigga, what kind of shit is that? If we're at war, my objective is you. That means I'm going to use any and every leverage I have at my disposal to bait you.

Just ask Ms. Daniels. The old bitch is butt-ass naked, tied to a chair in her very own dining room, with a dirty sock shoved down her throat as a gag. Her old saggy titties, keep shaking up and down as her chest rises and falls from crying.

Ms. Daniels is that nigga Murda's grandma. She raised Murda after his mother ran off years ago to chase the dope sack. Murda could not possibly love this woman, because at the very first mention of war, she should've been protected if he had love for her.

Now, some niggaz may say I'm wrong. After pistol whip-ping and torturing her, I made her call Murda and tell him to come home. Naaw, I'm not wrong, I'm just using what I got to my advantage. Everybody's got a weakness. All you gotta do is find it.

Her tears were all it took. At the sound of hearing her cry, he vowed to come kill me. It was hilarious. Here I was beating his grandma and he was swearing to God he was going to kill me.

Speaking of the devil, Murda pulled up in front of the house no later than fifteen minutes after I called him. I watched through the front window as he crossed the lawn.

"Look Ella May, our little Xavier is home," I taunted Ms. Daniels for the fuck of it.

Murda came bursting through the door like he was really going to save the day. He had his gun in his hands. The problem was I was standing directly behind Ms. Daniels with a big ass .357 pointed at the back of the bitch's head.

"Come on now, killah, you bust through the door like you're 'bout to get off into some gangsta shit. It ain't going down like that, playboy." I shoved the barrel into her head for emphasis. "The first thing you're gonna do is drop the banger if you want this old bitch to live."

For a minute, he looked like he wanted to say fuck his grandma and go all *Smoking Aces* up in this bitch. But then he listened to reason I guess because he dropped the gun and closed the door.

"Xavier what's going on? Who's this monster?" I don't know how the gag came out of her mouth, but I picked it up and made sure to shove it further down her old wretched throat.

"Big Mama, it's okay, this will all be over in a moment. Don't you worry." Murda was right about that. It will be over soon. He tried his best to avert his eyes from her nakedness when he talked to her. Not me, I slapped one of her tits.

"Yeah, Big Mama, don't you worry yo pretty little head unless you want me to knock you upside it again, or maybe you want me to make you feel nineteen again."

Murda took a step towards me. I cocked my .357. "Try me, nigga!" I told him.

I wouldn't hesitate to set his grandma's noodles on her sleeve and see what she was thinking. A bullet to the back of her head with this .357 would do just that.

"Now strip, nigga! Come on, Murda, take it off. Either take it all off or show me what that Murda shit is all about." It was a treat teasing the young killah.

He knew he didn't have a choice. He reluctantly came out his clothes, but he did it.

"Damn, Grandma! You see what the little mothafucka is working with? I bet Grandpa had a totem pole, huh, Grandma? You used to get yo old ass up on that big ole dick and have a field day, didn't you?" I couldn't help myself. It was funny and I was having fun.

I turned my attention back towards Murda. "You and your boys have really been giving me a real fucking headache."

"Fuck you, punk! You know what time it is. It's all Gas or nothin! Hurry up and do what you got to do!"

Ms. Daniels was squirming and trying to say something. Probably rebuking her grandson for his foul language.

"Do what I got to do. Nigga, do you think this is a game? Do what I got to do…"

Boom!

I pointed the .357 at Ms. Daniels' thigh and put a whole the size of Kansas in that bitch. To her credit, the old hag didn't make that much noise.

"Tell me where Dollar-Sign lay his head and I'll let grandma go. You're deader than a doorknob regardless. But I give you my word, I'll let Grandma live."

I was expecting Murda to talk a little shit before he went out. What I wasn't fucking expecting is what actually happened. This nigga dove on the floor, picked his gun up and rolled like some Universal Studios stuntman shit.

Bocca! Bocca! Bocca!

Holy shit! This little mothafucka was sending hot shit at me. Two of his bullets hit his grandma. One caught her in her throat and the other one knocked her shit out of her thinking cap. The third bullet whizzed so close by my face; I felt the heat from the slug.

Boom! Boom! Boom! Boom!

I let the .357 talk. Trust and believe, my aim stay on point. Two of the slugs from the .357 caught Murda in the chest. Another smacked in the floor next to him. The last slug hit him in his mouth.

Police sirens were close, so I slapped a speed reloader in and walked to stand over him.

"Revenge Is Promised, right?" I asked him.

Boom! Boom! Boom! Boom!

"It sure is!"

There wasn't any way in hell that Mudra would walk away from that shit. I didn't have time to ponder it. As I was reloading, police cars pulled up front.

"Fuck!" I was frustrated but I didn't panic. In fact, I sent one more slug into Murda's head just because.

The police were filing out of their squad cars as I was headed out the back door. While they surrounded the front of the house, I was jumping the backyard gate into the neighbor's yard.

I got my second shock for the day. Right next to the swimming pool, a couple was butt naked going at it. A white couple. The chick was a big tit, big booty redhead, who had her head down while she was getting fucked hard from behind.

Dude had an oil-tanned, Bruce Lee, karate body. His eyes were closed while he gave the redhead all he had. I mean, he was giving it to her. Had the circumstances been different, I would've stayed and watched. I don't know if I was shocked or impressed. All them gunshots that just went off no more than fifty feet away and here they are still fucking, with no worries.

As it was, them people were close. So, I had to do it moving. I walked right on by, keeping my eye on them the entire time. Walked into the house and found a set of BMW keys right on the counter. The couple never saw me. I walked right out the front door like I owned the house, or at least like I belonged in it. The BMW was a big body, and it was parked right there in the driveway. I was just hoping it wasn't a stick shift. If it was, I couldn't drive it. I would be forced to drive the Toyota Prius that was next to it.

I unlocked the smoke gray BMW and saw it was an automatic. I started her right up and drove away, mapping out the details for my text target. Before it's all said and done, I'm going to murder every single last one of them little mothafuckas.

"Talking about some Gas Nation shit. Fuck Gas Nation, I'm a Decepticon, bitch!" I yelled out as I drove off down the street.

I drove right past a squad car that never looked in my direction, it was busy speeding to get into position to seal the area off.

Me? I'm gone!

De'Kari

CHAPTER 20

Two nights before

The doctor didn't want to move the sheet down to reveal Jeff's head, due to the gunshots. But I wasn't hearing any of that shit. I was a street nigga. A few bullet wounds weren't going to get to me. I needed to see my nigga.

When I pulled the sheet down, I felt sick to my stomach. Half of my nigga'z face was blown off. Shit looked painful as fuck. I just stared at my nigga'z lifeless body, wishing I would've been there with him.

I wouldn't let myself get all soft and sentimental and shit. No, I was too Gas'd up for that. I was done playing games with this nigga Ty'Reese. It was time to show him how Gas Nation rolled. Time to show him how I rolled.

When I turned to look at the doctor, he took a step backwards. I guess I looked that evil.

"Yeah, that's my brother, Doc." After signing some forms, left the morgue.

Everybody was right where I left them in the waiting scan of the E.R. I didn't stop or slow down. I stormed right out of the hospital and the Gas Nation followed behind me. When we got outside, a tow truck was towing my brother's truck. I knew the police was taking it in for evidence. Still, I wanted to tell the tow truck driver to drop my brother's shit back down and do it moving. I refused to let myself get side-tracked.

I waited for us to get to the far side of the parking lot to make sure it was only us around. Then I addressed my squad.

"I want everybody to listen to me carefully. We've taken some major hits to our organization. Mothafucka's getting at us like shit is sweet or something around this bitch! This mothafucka Ty'Reese has gone too far. What he did to Tasha was the worst kind of disrespect. But now I just had to go look at my big brother on a metal slab with half of his fucking head blown off.

"I'm tired of this mothafucka! I want this bitch-ass nigga'z head cut off and delivered to me! I want something so bad done to this nigga, that a mothafucka would rather cross his mama than to fuck with our mothafuck'n family. Tonight, I want any and every fucking Decepticon knocked the fuck down! I want this nigga Ty'Reese found! And I want every last fucking trap house we got, shut the fuck down, until this shit is done! This ain't a game, if you niggaz want that Gas Nation's money, then I need to see you can earn the name Gas Nation! Burn this bitch down!"

I was so excited I was sweating. A nigga had to calm the fuck down before I hyperventilated. After my semi-speech I climbed back in the Nova. C1ty climbed back into the passenger seat. There wasn't a need to say anything more to the team. If shutting niggaz' money down didn't get their attention, then I didn't know what the fuck would.

"How are you trying to go about this, big bro?" he asked me as we pulled out of the parking lot.

"C1ty, I want the city of Oakland to bleed Damu red out in this bitch." I know I had to come up with a plan. I just didn't know what.

"What about the Mexican homies? It might just be time to bring in some new blood and fresh faces. Plus, them two mothafuckas seem to be B.T.A.," he responded back to me.

"You know what? You're right, cousin. Face did call and say he was on deck if we needed him." Right now, I don't give a fuck how it may look calling for help. I just wanted Ty'Reese.

I picked up my cell phone and hit Face up.

"Dollar-Sign, what's up, my nigga?" Face answered on the second ring.

"Shit's kind of ugly around my side of town. Face, I ain't even 'bout to lie to you, homie. A nigga just now leaving the morgue, seeing my nigga all fucked up laid out on a mothafuck'n platter. I need to put on end to this shit, my nigga."

"Say less, my nigga, I got you. I'm gonna come through tomorrow with that nigga Fat Boy and holla at you on some up close and personal shit, my nigga." The sound of his voice told me it was something more to what he was saying.

"Aaight, bet that! I'll see you tomorrow!" I hung up the phone.

"Face and Fat Boy gonna slide through tomorrow so we can holla about some shit. Blood, I really hope we find this mothafucka soon," I said to C1ty.

"Trust me, cousin, we're gonna find this mothafucka. I mean, a nigga can't hide forever."

"Let's hope you're right."

*** 3X ***

A week later

It was a hellavah turn out for Tasha and Jeff To Da Left's funerals. A nigga ain't waste no expenses. Everything was the best a nigga could find. From the floral arrangements to the caskets, I made sure they went off with a bang, in the best. Tasha and the baby's casket were a lavender and white combination, with chrome trimming. The inside was all silk. Jeff's coffin was black and gold to salute the young king that he was. I spared no expense. It cost a grip to get Jennifer Hudson to sing during the ceremony, but it was worth every penny.

I'd lost two brothers and my sister, and because of that, the city of Oakland was brought to its knees. As an answer to my call, there've been more than five murders a night ever since Jeff To Da Left's death. The Decepticons were paying a heavy fucking price for the sins of their father. In just a week, close to forty of its members were killed.

From the way my team was going, there was no way in hell they intended to slow down or let up on the Decepticons any time soon. We were trying to annihilate all of them mothafuckas off the face of this earth. Then and only then could business ever go back to normal.

We were driving in the car and Clty handed me the lit blunt. The phat Backwood was filled with Gorilla Glue, some new shit taking the streets by storm. I took a hit and tried my best not to choke. The potent weed was like candy to niggaz. By my third hit, a nigga was already high as a kite.

Today was a good day, so I kept smoking. Next, I passed the blunt to Kane. He took one hit and said, "Damn cuzzo, what that nigga did to Murda's G'Mama was some cold shit. You know niggaz saying the sick mothafucka slept with the old Bird. Blood, that nigga is sick."

"Blood, that nigga ain't fuck that old bird, that's just niggaz talking shit. You know how niggaz do. But no matter what, the shit he did was foul. Tying her up, asshole butt naked and pistol whooped her. The old bird had to be in her seventies," Clty said from the passenger seat.

I turned the corner and began searching for the house we'd driven way out of the way to find.

"Regardless how old she was, mothafuckas are playing dirty pool and taking shit to a whole other level when they start bringing in women, period! I mean, this street shit, a mothafucka is supposed to leave it to those in the street. Fucking with nigga'z family, especially the women and children, is out of pocket. But that's why this nigga gonna get what the fuck he gets."

Finally, I found the house and pulled up in front of it.

"Are you niggaz ready for this shit?" I asked as I pulled out a big ass Desert Eagle .44 and my cell phone.

"You already know," C1ty responded.

"Let's go." The three of us climbed out of the Nova on our *Pulp Fiction* shit with guns out, cocked and loaded.

I punched a number into the phone and put it to my ears.

"Hello?" she answered right away.

"I'm here," was all I said. This could've been a set-up for all I know.

A few moments later, the front door opened. My niggaz and me were ready, Gas'd the fuck up. Two females exited the house. One was a little black girl who could not have been any older than sixteen. She looked familiar. The second chick looked like she was black mixed with some type of hybrid Latina, Asian or something. The little foreign bitch was bad as fuck.

I already knew it was the little girl I'd been speaking with. She had an interesting story to tell. It was worth listening to. It didn't mean it was real though.

"So, where he at?" was all I said.

The little one turned towards the open door and called out to him. It took her to call out three times before he came and peeked out the doorway. The way he peeked his head around the door made me think of when Queen Latifah did it in *Set It Off*.

Something about the way he kept poking his head out of the door frame and then ducking back behind it made me pause. There was something different, something unnatural about his behavior.

When the little girl who called herself, Ebony called his name for the fourth time, he came bolting out of the house, laughing and jumping up and down like a little kid.

"You've got to be fucking kidding me!" Kane's tone of disbelief clearly spoke what we were all thinking.

"This has got to be some type of joke. I say we smoke these two bitches for tryna play us pussy like this. There ain't no way in hell this little retarded mothafucka right there is Ty'Reese," C1ty called out.

But it was!

Even if I didn't hear or believe the story Ebony told me last night, I'd seen Ty'Reese enough times when we all lived in the Projects to know him when I saw him.

"Yeah, Kane, that's him. And that nigga ain't doing no kind of acting." As I said this, I lowered my Desert Eagle. I didn't tuck it away, because I still didn't know Ebony's angle.

"Okay, so you got us here and I see your work. But it's time for you to start talking and lay your cards out on the table."

*** **3X** ***

CHAPTER 21

EBONY

Three nights before…

I was laying across my bed doing homework and listening to Barack Obama give his *State of the Union* speech. I was impressed and happy that a Black man finally made it to the White House.

Even though I wasn't alive for slavery or segregation, I still witness the racism of today that was very much alive and in our faces. Nevertheless, it felt good to be able to take a moment out of my young life to enjoy and join in on this historical moment.

A gentle knock came at my bedroom door. "Who is it?" I called out.

"It's me, Alyanna."

"Come in."

She was barefoot. Her feet made no sound as she hurried across my room to my bed. She crossed the room like somebody who was up to no good and didn't want to get caught. Instantly I sat up.

"Hey Alyanna, what's up, girl?"

"Ebony, we need to talk," she said urgently.

"Where's my brother?" Ebony asked.

"He's outside talking on the phone. You know he doesn't talk around me. Something serious is going on though, because he keeps going outside to answer his ringing phone and he's smoking more than normal," Alyanna explained.

"Oh, okay, then stop acting so secretive and tell me what you want to talk about."

She gestured toward the bed, asking more for permission to sit on my bed. I gave it to her. She sat down and just stayed there for a minute getting her composure. After a couple of deep breaths, she looked at me and said, "I just got off the phone with my brother. He said it's time."

I just looked at her for a second. There was no need to say anything else.

Alyanna was Ty'Reese's, girlfriend. The two of them have been dating for over nine months now. She was Black, Japanese and Hispanic. Although you could barely see any resemblance of her Latina genes, it was that side of her that she embraced the most. Her brother happened to be her role model and idol. Alyanna would do anything for her brother.

"Okay, are you ready?" I started to get excited myself.

She and I have been talking about today for almost a month now. So, today was the day. I began to feel a nervous excitement building in my body, yet I refused to let it show and have her think that I was some scared little girl.

"Yeah, I'm ready. Everything is in order. I just wanted to let you know."

"Okay, thanks. I'll be ready." I told her, praying to God that would be true.

She leaned over and gave me a hug. A long tight hug. Then whispered in my ear, "Don't worry, Ebony, I got you."

After her little assurance, she got up and left. I tried to go back to what I was doing before she came, but I couldn't. I couldn't help but to think about it all. Before I knew it, the time had passed. It wasn't until the knock came to my door and Alyanna called out that it was time for dinner, that I realized how late it was.

Closing my homework, I cut off the TV, got up and went to wash up for dinner. All I could think of was the two people in my life that were taken from me. I missed them so much.

Tears began rolling down my cheeks, which I had to wipe away. Now was not the time to set off any alarms. Alyanna and Ty'Reese were already seated at the table when I walked in.

When I sat down, Ty'Reese asked me, "Did you get all of your homework done?"

"No, I was paying too much attention to Obama and his *State of the Union* speech."

"Okay, well after dinner, make sure you finish the rest of your homework. I was going to say we could've gone and balled after dinner, but I guess we'll do it tomorrow." After he said that, he dug into his plate of homemade enchiladas.

The rest of dinner went by in a blur. Before I knew it, Alyanna was pouring my brother a glass of Hennessy and lighting his blunt. It was a ritual. Every night after dinner he smoked a blunt and had his drink.

After lighting the blunt, she handed it to him. Ty'Reese took a good long drag and started choking like he was going to die. When the choking subsided, he grabbed his glass of Hennessy and took a big gulp.

"God damn! What the fuck is that?" he asked Alyanna. Although he was looking at her like she was crazy. The effects of the weed were kicking in already. He was impressed.

"That's that new Gorilla Glue everybody's talking about. I got you a pound of it from my brother." She talked as sexy as she could.

"Here, let me refill your glass for you, daddy."

Ty'Reese continued to smoke the blunt while we all talked about our day. About thirty minutes later and halfway into the second blunt, is when it happened.

First, he made a weird noise, then he got quiet. The look in his eyes was so distant and far away. I knew something was happening, I just didn't know what.

What I did know was Alyanna had successfully slipped him a Mickey in his Hennessy and gave him two KJ blunts. Either one of the three would fry Ty'Reese's brain. The three together would leave him completely sizzling. Ty'Reese had already smoked so many blunts by then, there was no way he could taste the faint flavor of the KJ in the blunt. When he was told the weed was Gorilla Glue, he greedily smoked it up.

While looking at him, I thought of the two people I've missed. The first was Mommy Valerie, the only mother that I knew. The second person I missed was Jeffrey. I was walking past the study one day, when I heard Ty'Reese in a drunken state, bragging about killing her and Jeffrey. I made him tell me everything. Considering he was drunk; it wasn't that difficult. Ty'Reese told me everything, starting with the fire.

Mama J. had told Jeffrey about me shortly after Jay was killed. He and I kicked it off immediately. Because of some things he had going on in the streets, he didn't want anyone to find out about me. Therefore, we kept our bond quiet.

I swore to get revenge for the people I loved and I'm keeping that promise to myself. One of the first things Jeffrey did for me was to make sure I had someone close that could protect me. When Alyanna first reached out to me on Facebook, I was hesitant until Jeffrey told me who she was.

Alyanna and I were friends long before Ty'Reese ever knew I existed. His fluke chance meeting Alyanna at the sandwich shop wasn't a fluke at all, it was carefully executed.

NARRATOR

Present Day

"Okay, so you got us here and I see your work. But it's time for you to start talking and lay your cards out on the table," Ty Dollar-Sign looked at Ebony and told her. Ty was thinking to himself how familiar she looked, she was the split image of Tasha.

Ty Dollar-Sign, C1ty and Kane were shocked when Ebony told them who she was. She followed that up with the story of everything that transpired over the last nine months, ending with Ty'Reese drinking the Mickey and smoking the weed laced with KJ that Alyanna ended up getting from her big brother. While Ebony had everyone's attention, Alyanna was privately sending a text message.

Ty Dollar-Sign was trying to figure out if the story was believable. On the one hand, she did look like Tasha's little twin mini-me. That, and given all the molestation that was going on inside the church, it was possible that she could be his little sister. Learning that it was Ty'Reese who really killed Jay and how Mama J. had succumbed to the blackmail out of fear of losing Ebony, it was all quite believable.

C1ty and Kane were also just shocked at how twisted this whole little ordeal was. To think all the killing and bloodshed was all behind Jeff To Da Left killing his mother all those years ago.

While they were talking, a Mercedes pulled up. Ty Dollar-Sign and the fellas drew their guns, wondering what was going on as the strange car parked. It turned out to be Scarface and Fat Boy, so they lowered their guns as the two of them emerged from the vehicle.

Alyanna walked up to Fat Boy and said something in Spanish, before giving her big brother a hug and a kiss on the cheek. The looks on the three goons' faces was priceless.

While Ty'Reese played in the front yard like a five-year-old kid, Alyanna and Fat Boy filled everyone in on the rest of the tale, then finished up with the meeting Ty Dollar-Sign had with Fat Boy and Scarface. They agreed to take care of Ty'Reese for him as a favor.

Dollar-Sign was so caught up in the losses they took and the funerals, that he forgot about the meeting with the two homies the other day.

Right now, twenty-nine-year-old Ty'Reese had the mind of a five-year-old, special needs kid as he ran around the front yard, playing with an imaginary friend. Everyone in the front yard watched in amazed disbelief.

It was the worst thing to experience, being alive but not being there mentally. Not remembering the life he had, not being able to intelligently enjoy his everyday experiences, he was lost within himself.

"What do you wanna to do to him?" Kane looked at Ty Dollar-Sign and asked.

Ty thought about killing Ty'Reese right there were he stood, but the sadistic side of him took over.

He turned to Scarface and Fat Boy. "Good looking homies, I owe you two niggaz big. Come by the trap tomorrow and I got you."

"Aight, my nigga, say less." They both turned to leave.

Ebony turned to Ty Dollar-Sign and spoke, "Whatever decision you make, just know this. I've been Gas Nation now for nine months and I don't plan on that changing. Older brother or not, I'm far from a punk." He couldn't help but to smirk. Everyone else was impressed by Ebony's bluntness.

Ty Dollar-Sign turned towards his vehicle, followed by C1ty and Kane. Then he told Ebony, "Come on, I got you." That was all he said.

Alyanna and Ebony followed the Nova in Alyanna's Lexus, with Ty'Reese in the back seat. Neither of them knew their destination, but they knew that they were heading towards San Francisco. Alyanna wondered just what the young killah had up his sleeve.

Driving down Market Street, both C1ty and Kane were quietly smoking their own individual blunts, wondering what was what. C1ty didn't care as much as Kane, because once they crossed over the Bay Bridge, they were back on his stomping grounds. Especially as they drove down Market Street in the Tenderloin.

From Market Street, they ended up switching over to Mission Street. "You gone tell us where we headed brah, or what?" Kane finally spoke up and asked.

"Right here," Ty Dollar-Sign replied as he pulled over. They were on the corner of 16th and Mission, the lowest of the slums. The bottom of the bottoms. Skid-fucking row!

"Right here?" Kane repeated. His hand clutched the Glock .40 that was on his lap.

"Fuck we gone do in the Mission District?" C1ty spoke up this time.

The Mission in San Francisco was like Times Square in New York back in the '80s, only twenty times grimier. It's where all the lowlifes come to get their hustle on, where the dope fiends came for their next fix, and where the police wanted to avoid at all costs.

"Come on," was all Ty Dollar-Sign said, before stepping out of the Nova.

Everybody was thinking about their own selfish scheme when they saw the two expensive cars pull up. They were on alert, hungrily staring to see who got out the vehicle. When the doors opened and three niggaz stepped out of the Nova, with big ass cannons in their hands and mugs on their faces, everyone scattered like roaches.

"What are we doing?" Alyanna asked as she came walking up to the trio.

"We're leaving him here. Right in the heart of Fuckville, USA. Take him inside that Burger King, give him five dollars and leave his bitch ass right there," he instructed her.

Alyanna followed his instructions. Everybody watched the beautiful woman that walked with the retarded man. The Mission District was full of scoundrels, misfits and rogues. Nobody would feel sorry for him or his condition here. Down in the Mission, everyone would see him as prey and take advantage of him in one way or the other. Every day would be a living hell. If they would've released him in Downtown Oakland or somewhere, he stood the chance of someone recognizing him or feeling sorry for him and showing him some kind of mercy.

By leaving him in the city, he was in a place where niggaz didn't give two fucks about nothing but their own. Sometimes, not even that.

Ty'Reese had a puzzling, stupid look on his face as Alyanna left him standing there in the middle of Burger King, holding on to a twenty-dollar bill. Something was off, but his mind wouldn't register what.

"Pretty lady go b-bye-bye," he mumbled as Alyanna and Ebony got back into the Lexus and followed Jeff to Da Left as he pulled off.

Ty'Reese just stood there repeating to himself, "Pretty lady go bye-bye," until a homeless man passing by saw the twenty-dollar bill. Without hesitation, the homeless man punched Ty'Reese as hard as he could in the jaw. The force of the blow dropped Ty'Reese, causing him to drop the money. The homeless man then kicked Ty'Reese hard in the stomach, which caused him to cry out.

The homeless man then picked up the money and went on about his business like nothing ever happened. He walked up to the counter and bought a number four with an extra order of French fries and a Whopper with cheese. The cashier learned a long time ago to mind her business, therefore she rang up the order like nothing had happened. People that watched the scene unfold were jealous, and mad that it wasn't them that acted fast and took the money from the gimp.

Ty'Reese just lay on the floor crying like a four-year-old, but he couldn't figure out why. He didn't understand.

Crazy!

*** **3X** ***

Six months later...

Ebony left the cemetery with tears rolling down her cheeks and her heart broken. Today was the third time in a month that she had been to the cemetery. She and Jeffrey hadn't known each other particularly long, but the bond the two of them shared meant the world to Ebony.

Growing up, Ebony always wished that she had siblings. Jefferey finding her was a dream come true. The day she found out about his death was the second worst day of her young life. Her mother's murder was the worst.

Ebony cried as she guided her car across the Bay Bridge, determined to make things right once and for all. Turning onto Mission Street in San Francisco, she reached into the center console for her cell phone. She punched in a set of numbers and waited while the phone rang. After the third ring, the person on the other end answered in a raspy, cigarette smoking voice. There was a brief exchange of words and the call ended.

Ebony continued driving on Mission Street until she came to 16th Street. She made a left onto 16th and a few blocks later, she spotted Capo Street. She made a right on Capo. Capo was a long alleyway that ran parallel to Mission. It was dark and grimy. A regular hangout for the lowlifes.

She slowed down and looked around for her contact. As she was looking, her phone started ringing. She pushed the answer button on her steering column and the call came through her speakers.

"Is that you that just turned into the alleyway?" the caller asked.

"Yeah, I'm in the black Porsche Cayenne," Ebony replied.

"Okay, I see you. I'm about thirty yards up the alleyway if you just keep coming straight. Do you see me waving? I'm in a Louis Vuitton skirt outfit and shoes.

"Yeah girl, I see you."

"Okay pull up." The phone call ended.

All eyes were on the foreign truck as it pulled into the alley way. The dope boys were curious to see if it was a big money spender. The dope fiends were hoping it was an easy come-up. When the truck stopped, everyone waited to see who would emerge from behind the tinted windows.

When Ebony stepped out the Porsche with her long Fendi trench coat on, all everyone paid attention to was the nickel plated 9mm she was clutching in her hand. Instantly, everyone found some business and got the fuck up out of hers.

Her contact walked up to her smiling and gave her a hug.

"Girl, give me a hug. You stepping out of the truck on some *Lara Croft Tomb Raider* shit!"

"Naaw more like the female in *New Jack City* that was killing people."

"Anyway, he's right over there by the dumpster."

Ebony looked over to where she was pointing and saw him right away. She reached into her pocket and pulled out a fat envelope filled with hundred-dollar bills and handed it to her.

"You might wanna leave, girl," Ebony told her as she grabbed the envelope.

Revenge was a dish best served cold, and today was payday.

She didn't wait for a response. Ebony walked over to her target and stood over him.

"I bet you thought you were going to get off that easy. Like you could kill my fucking brother and be allowed to run the streets like shit was sweet. You got the game fucked up, Ty'Reese. *REVENGE IS PROMISED*, nigga, and karma is a mothafucka!" With that, she pointed her 9mm at his left kneecap.

Boc! Boc!

She fired. Both shots crashed into his kneecap.

No one moved as Ty'Reese howled in pain. Gunshots were nothing new in the mean streets of San Francisco. They were a daily occurrence in this part of the neighborhood.

Ebony aimed at the other leg and fired two shots into that leg as well. There was no way in hell Ty'Reese would be going anywhere anytime soon. She walked over to the back of the Porsche and retrieved a gas can. Just as calm as day, she walked back over to a now whimpering and shaking Ty'Reese, and began dousing him with the gasoline.

The spectators couldn't believe what they were seeing. The young lady looked too beautiful to be doing something so heinous, yet here she was, displaying pure evil right in front of them. As she poured the gasoline, they excitedly made bets between themselves if she would go through with it and set the poor bastard on fire.

When Ebony pulled a lighter out of her coat pocket, everyone in the alley became silent. She struck the Zippo lighter with her gloved hand and threw the lighter on Ty'Reese's body. Instantly, he was engulfed with flames.

The loud, soul piercing shriek that emitted from his mouth sounded animalistic. Numb to any pain he might be feeling, Ebony sat and watched him suffer for a while, lost in the savory taste of revenge. She just stood there with a sick sadistic smile on her face.

When Ty Dollar-Sign said they were going to leave Ty'Reese to roam free and suffer from their imposed retardation on him, she thought that Ty Dollar-Sign had lost his natural rabid ass mind.

Her brother, Jeff To Da Left, was all Gas Nation and he was super turnt the fuck up! And that's exactly how Ebony intended to be... "All Gas, No Brakes!"

She walked back to her Porsche and drove off, listening to Jeff To Da Left's 3X Krazy CD with a smile on her face!

To Be Continued...
3X Krazy 3
REVENGE IS PROMISED
Coming Soon

Submission Guideline

Submit the first three chapters of your completed manuscript to ldpsubmissions@gmail.com, subject line: Your book's title. The manuscript must be in a .doc file and sent as an attachment. Document should be in Times New Roman, double spaced and in size 12 font. Also, provide your synopsis and full contact information. If sending multiple submissions, they must each be in a separate email.

Have a story but no way to send it electronically? You can still submit to LDP/Ca$h Presents. Send in the first three chapters, written or typed, of your completed manuscript to:

LDP: Submissions Dept
Po Box 944
Stockbridge, Ga 30281

DO NOT send original manuscript. Must be a duplicate.

Provide your synopsis and a cover letter containing your full contact information.

Thanks for considering LDP and Ca$h Presents.

<u>Coming Soon from Lock Down Publications/Ca$h Presents</u>

BOW DOWN TO MY GANGSTA

By **Ca$h**

TORN BETWEEN TWO

By **Coffee**

THE STREETS STAINED MY SOUL **II**

By **Marcellus Allen**

BLOOD OF A BOSS **VI**

SHADOWS OF THE GAME II

By **Askari**

LOYAL TO THE GAME **IV**

By **T.J. & Jelissa**

IF LOVING YOU IS WRONG… **III**

By **Jelissa**

TRUE SAVAGE **VIII**

MIDNIGHT CARTEL III

DOPE BOY MAGIC IV

CITY OF KINGZ II

By **Chris Green**

BLAST FOR ME **III**

A SAVAGE DOPEBOY III

CUTTHROAT MAFIA III

DUFFLE BAG CARTEL VI

By **Ghost**

A HUSTLER'S DECEIT III

KILL ZONE **II**

BAE BELONGS TO ME III

A DOPE BOY'S QUEEN III

By **Aryanna**

COKE KINGS V

KING OF THE TRAP II

By **T.J. Edwards**

GORILLAZ IN THE BAY V

3X KRAZY III

De'Kari

THE STREETS ARE CALLING II

Duquie Wilson

KINGPIN KILLAZ IV

STREET KINGS III

PAID IN BLOOD III

CARTEL KILLAZ IV

DOPE GODS III

Hood Rich

SINS OF A HUSTLA II

ASAD

KINGZ OF THE GAME VI

Playa Ray

SLAUGHTER GANG IV

RUTHLESS HEART IV

By Willie Slaughter

THE HEART OF A SAVAGE III

By Jibril Williams

FUK SHYT II

By Blakk Diamond

TRAP QUEEN

By Troublesome

YAYO V

GHOST MOB II

Stilloan Robinson

KINGPIN DREAMS III

By Paper Boi Rari

CREAM II

By Yolanda Moore

SON OF A DOPE FIEND III

By Renta

FOREVER GANGSTA II

GLOCKS ON SATIN SHEETS III

By Adrian Dulan

LOYALTY AIN'T PROMISED III

By Keith Williams

THE PRICE YOU PAY FOR LOVE II

By Destiny Skai

I'M NOTHING WITHOUT HIS LOVE II

SINS OF A THUG II

By Monet Dragun

LIFE OF A SAVAGE IV

MURDA SEASON IV

GANGLAND CARTEL III

CHI'RAQ GANGSTAS II

By **Romell Tukes**

QUIET MONEY IV

THUG LIFE II

EXTENDED CLIP II

By **Trai'Quan**

THE STREETS MADE ME III

By **Larry D. Wright**

IF YOU CROSS ME ONCE II

ANGEL III

By **Anthony Fields**

FRIEND OR FOE III

By **Mimi**

SAVAGE STORMS II

By **Meesha**

BLOOD ON THE MONEY III

By J-Blunt

THE STREETS WILL NEVER CLOSE II

By K'ajji

NIGHTMARES OF A HUSTLA III

By King Dream

THE WIFEY I USED TO BE II

By Nicole Goosby

IN THE ARM OF HIS BOSS

By Jamila

MONEY, MURDER & MEMORIES II

Malik D. Rice

CONCRETE KILLAZ II

By Kingpen

HARD AND RUTHLESS II

By Von Wiley Hall

LEVELS TO THIS SHYT II

By Ah'Million

Available Now

RESTRAINING ORDER **I & II**

By **CA$H & Coffee**

LOVE KNOWS NO BOUNDARIES **I II & III**

By **Coffee**

RAISED AS A GOON I, II, III & IV

BRED BY THE SLUMS I, II, III

BLAST FOR ME I & II

ROTTEN TO THE CORE I II III

A BRONX TALE I, II, III

DUFFLE BAG CARTEL I II III IV V

HEARTLESS GOON I II III IV

A SAVAGE DOPEBOY I II

HEARTLESS GOON I II III

DRUG LORDS I II III

CUTTHROAT MAFIA I II

By **Ghost**

LAY IT DOWN **I & II**

LAST OF A DYING BREED I II

BLOOD STAINS OF A SHOTTA I & II III

By **Jamaica**

LOYAL TO THE GAME I II III

LIFE OF SIN I, II III

By **TJ & Jelissa**

BLOODY COMMAS I & II

SKI MASK CARTEL I II & III

KING OF NEW YORK I II,III IV V

RISE TO POWER I II III

COKE KINGS I II III IV

BORN HEARTLESS I II III IV

KING OF THE TRAP

By **T.J. Edwards**

IF LOVING HIM IS WRONG...I & II

LOVE ME EVEN WHEN IT HURTS I II III

By **Jelissa**

WHEN THE STREETS CLAP BACK I & II III

THE HEART OF A SAVAGE I II

By **Jibril Williams**

A DISTINGUISHED THUG STOLE MY HEART I II & III

LOVE SHOULDN'T HURT I II III IV

RENEGADE BOYS I II III IV

PAID IN KARMA I II III

SAVAGE STORMS

By **Meesha**

A GANGSTER'S CODE I &, II III

A GANGSTER'S SYN I II III

THE SAVAGE LIFE I II III

CHAINED TO THE STREETS I II III

BLOOD ON THE MONEY I II

By J-Blunt

PUSH IT TO THE LIMIT

By **Bre' Hayes**

BLOOD OF A BOSS **I, II, III, IV, V**

SHADOWS OF THE GAME

By **Askari**

THE STREETS BLEED MURDER **I, II & III**

THE HEART OF A GANGSTA I II& III

By **Jerry Jackson**

CUM FOR ME I II III IV V VI

An **LDP Erotica Collaboration**

BRIDE OF A HUSTLA **I II & II**

THE FETTI GIRLS **I, II& III**

CORRUPTED BY A GANGSTA I, II III, IV

BLINDED BY HIS LOVE

THE PRICE YOU PAY FOR LOVE

DOPE GIRL MAGIC I II III

By **Destiny Skai**

WHEN A GOOD GIRL GOES BAD

By **Adrienne**

THE COST OF LOYALTY I II III

By Kweli

A GANGSTER'S REVENGE **I II III & IV**

THE BOSS MAN'S DAUGHTERS I II III IV V

A SAVAGE LOVE **I & II**

BAE BELONGS TO ME I II

A HUSTLER'S DECEIT I, II, III

WHAT BAD BITCHES DO I, II, III

SOUL OF A MONSTER I II III

KILL ZONE

A DOPE BOY'S QUEEN I II

By **Aryanna**

A KINGPIN'S AMBITON

A KINGPIN'S AMBITION **II**

I MURDER FOR THE DOUGH

By **Ambitious**

TRUE SAVAGE I II III IV V VI VII

DOPE BOY MAGIC I, II, III

MIDNIGHT CARTEL I II

CITY OF KINGZ

By **Chris Green**

A DOPEBOY'S PRAYER

By **Eddie "Wolf" Lee**

THE KING CARTEL **I, II & III**

By **Frank Gresham**

THESE NIGGAS AIN'T LOYAL **I, II & III**

By **Nikki Tee**

GANGSTA SHYT **I II &III**

By **CATO**

THE ULTIMATE BETRAYAL

By **Phoenix**

BOSS'N UP **I , II & III**

By **Royal Nicole**

I LOVE YOU TO DEATH

By Destiny J

I RIDE FOR MY HITTA

I STILL RIDE FOR MY HITTA

By **Misty Holt**

LOVE & CHASIN' PAPER

By **Qay Crockett**

TO DIE IN VAIN

SINS OF A HUSTLA

By **ASAD**

BROOKLYN HUSTLAZ

By **Boogsy Morina**

BROOKLYN ON LOCK I & II

By **Sonovia**

GANGSTA CITY

By **Teddy Duke**

A DRUG KING AND HIS DIAMOND I & II III

A DOPEMAN'S RICHES

HER MAN, MINE'S TOO I, II

CASH MONEY HO'S

THE WIFEY I USED TO BE

By Nicole Goosby

TRAPHOUSE KING **I II & III**

KINGPIN KILLAZ I II III

STREET KINGS I II

PAID IN BLOOD **I II**

CARTEL KILLAZ I II III

DOPE GODS I II

By **Hood Rich**

LIPSTICK KILLAH **I, II, III**

CRIME OF PASSION I II & III

FRIEND OR FOE I II

By **Mimi**

STEADY MOBBN' **I, II, III**

THE STREETS STAINED MY SOUL

By **Marcellus Allen**

WHO SHOT YA **I, II, III**

SON OF A DOPE FIEND I II

Renta

GORILLAZ IN THE BAY **I II III IV**

TEARS OF A GANGSTA I II

3X KRAZY I II

DE'KARI

TRIGGADALE I II III

Elijah R. Freeman

GOD BLESS THE TRAPPERS I, II, III

THESE SCANDALOUS STREETS I, II, III

FEAR MY GANGSTA I, II, III IV, V

THESE STREETS DON'T LOVE NOBODY I, II

BURY ME A G I, II, III, IV, V

A GANGSTA'S EMPIRE I, II, III, IV

THE DOPEMAN'S BODYGAURD I II

THE REALEST KILLAZ I II III

Tranay Adams
THE STREETS ARE CALLING
Duquie Wilson
MARRIED TO A BOSS... I II III
By Destiny Skai & Chris Green
KINGZ OF THE GAME I II III IV V
Playa Ray
SLAUGHTER GANG I II III
RUTHLESS HEART I II III
By Willie Slaughter
FUK SHYT
By Blakk Diamond
DON'T F#CK WITH MY HEART I II
By Linnea
ADDICTED TO THE DRAMA I II III
IN THE ARM OF HIS BOSS II
By Jamila
YAYO I II III IV
A SHOOTER'S AMBITION I II
By S. Allen
TRAP GOD I II III
By Troublesome
FOREVER GANGSTA
GLOCKS ON SATIN SHEETS I II
By Adrian Dulan
TOE TAGZ I II III
LEVELS TO THIS SHYT

By Ah'Million

KINGPIN DREAMS I II

By Paper Boi Rari

CONFESSIONS OF A GANGSTA I II III

By Nicholas Lock

I'M NOTHING WITHOUT HIS LOVE

SINS OF A THUG

By Monet Dragun

CAUGHT UP IN THE LIFE I II III

By Robert Baptiste

NEW TO MONEY, MURDER & MEMORIES

THE GAME I II III

By **Malik D. Rice**

LIFE OF A SAVAGE I II III

A GANGSTA'S QUR'AN I II III

MURDA SEASON I II III

GANGLAND CARTEL I II

CHI'RAQ GANGSTAS

By **Romell Tukes**

LOYALTY AIN'T PROMISED I II

By Keith Williams

QUIET MONEY I II III

THUG LIFE

EXTENDED CLIP

By **Trai'Quan**

THE STREETS MADE ME I II

By **Larry D. Wright**

THE ULTIMATE SACRIFICE I, II, III, IV, V, VI
KHADIFI
IF YOU CROSS ME ONCE
ANGEL I II
By **Anthony Fields**
THE LIFE OF A HOOD STAR
By **Ca$h & Rashia Wilson**
THE STREETS WILL NEVER CLOSE
By **K'ajji**
CREAM
By **Yolanda Moore**
NIGHTMARES OF A HUSTLA I II
By **King Dream**
CONCRETE KILLAZ
By **Kingpen**
HARD AND RUTHLESS
By **Von Wiley Hall**
GHOST MOB II
Stilloan Robinson

BOOKS BY LDP'S CEO, CA$H

TRUST IN NO MAN

TRUST IN NO MAN 2

TRUST IN NO MAN 3

BONDED BY BLOOD

SHORTY GOT A THUG

THUGS CRY

THUGS CRY 2

THUGS CRY 3

TRUST NO BITCH

TRUST NO BITCH 2

TRUST NO BITCH 3

TIL MY CASKET DROPS

RESTRAINING ORDER

RESTRAINING ORDER 2

IN LOVE WITH A CONVICT

LIFE OF A HOOD STAR

De'Kari

Printed in the USA
CPSIA information can be obtained
at www.ICGtesting.com
LVHW021323250823
756180LV00006B/468